I0818799

Maiwa's Revenge

or The War of the Little Hand

Maiwa's Revenge

or The War of the Little Hand

by H. Rider Haggard

Start Publishing PD LLC

Manufactured in the United States of America

Cover art: Shutterstock/Taisiya Kozorez

Cover design: Jennifer Do

10 9 8 7 6 5 4 3 2 1

ISBN 979-8-8809-0143-2

Table of Contents

Preface

It may be well to state that the incident of the "Thing that bites" recorded in this tale is not an effort of the imagination. On the contrary, it is "plagiarized." Mandara, a well-known chief on the east coast of Africa, has such an article, *and uses it*. In the same way the wicked conduct attributed to Wambe is not without a precedent. T'Chaka, the Zulu Napoleon, never allowed a child of his to live. Indeed he went further, for on discovering that his mother, Unandi, was bringing up one of his sons in secret, like Nero he killed her, and with his own hand.

Gobo Strikes

One day—it was about a week after Allan Quatermain told me his story of the "Three Lions," and of the moving death of Jim-Jim—he and I were walking home together on the termination of a day's shooting. He owned about two thousand acres of shooting round the place he had bought in Yorkshire, over a hundred of which were wood. It was the second year of his occupation of the estate, and already he had reared a very fair head of pheasants, for he was an all-round sportsman, and as fond of shooting with a shot-gun as with an eight-bore rifle. We were three guns that day, Sir Henry Curtis, Old Quatermain, and myself; but Sir Henry was obliged to leave in the middle of the afternoon in order to meet his agent, and inspect an outlying farm where a new shed was wanted. However, he was coming back to dinner, and going to bring Captain Good with him, for Brayley Hall was not more than two miles from the Grange.

We had met with very fair sport, considering that we were only going through outlying cover for cocks. I think that we had killed twenty- seven, a woodcock and a leash of partridges which we secured out of a driven covey. On our way home there lay a long narrow spinney, which was a very favourite "lie" for woodcocks, and generally held a pheasant or two as well.

"Well, what do you say?" said old Quatermain, "shall we beat through this for a finish?"

I assented, and he called to the keeper who was following with a little knot of beaters, and told him to beat the spinney.

"Very well, sir," answered the man, "but it's getting wonderful dark, and the wind's rising a gale. It will take you all your time to hit a woodcock if the spinney holds one."

"You show us the woodcocks, Jeffries," answered Quatermain quickly, for he never liked being crossed in anything to do with sport, "and we will look after shooting them."

The man turned and went rather sulkily. I heard him say to the under- keeper, "He's pretty good, the master is, I'm not saying he isn't, but if he kills a woodcock in this light and wind, I'm a Dutchman."

I think that Quatermain heard him too, though he said nothing. The wind was rising every minute, and by the time the beat begun it blew big guns. I stood at the right-hand corner of the spinney, which curved round somewhat, and Quatermain stood at the left, about forty paces from me. Presently an old cock pheasant came rocketing over me, looking as though the feathers were being blown out of his tail. I missed him clean with the first barrel, and was never more pleased with myself in my life than when I doubled him up with the second, for the shot was not an easy one. In the faint light I could see Quatermain nodding his head in approval, when through the groaning of the trees I heard the shouts of the beaters, "Cock forward, cock to the right." Then came a whole volley of shouts, "Woodcock to the right," "Cock to the left," "Cock over."

I looked up, and presently caught sight of one of the woodcocks coming down the wind upon me like a flash. In that dim light I could not follow all his movements as he zigzagged through the naked tree-tops; indeed I could see him when his wings flitted up. Now he was passing me—*bang*, and a flick of the wing, I had missed him; *bang* again. Surely he was down; no, there he went to my left.

"Cock to you," I shouted, stepping forward so as to get Quatermain between me and the faint angry light of the dying day, for I wanted to see if he would "wipe my eye." I knew him to be a wonderful shot, but I thought that cock would puzzle him.

I saw him raise his gun ever so little and bend forward, and at that moment out flashed two woodcocks into the open, the one I had missed to his right, and the other to his left.

At the same time a fresh shout arose of, "Woodcock over," and looking down the spinney I saw a third bird high up in the air, being blown along like a brown and whirling leaf straight over Quatermain's head. And then followed the prettiest little bit of shooting that I ever saw. The bird to the right was flying low, not ten yards from the line of a hedgerow, and Quatermain took him first because he would become invisible the soonest of any. Indeed, nobody who had not his hawk's eyes could have seen to shoot at all. But he saw the bird well enough to kill it dead as a stone. Then turning sharply, he pulled on the second bird at about forty-five yards, and over he went. By this time the third woodcock was nearly over him, and flying very high, straight down the wind, a hundred feet up or more, I should say. I saw him glance at it as he opened his gun, threw out the right cartridge and slipped in another, turning round as he did so. By this time the cock was nearly fifty yards away from him, and travelling like a flash. Lifting his gun he fired after it, and, wonderful as the shot was, killed it dead. A tearing gust of wind caught the dead bird, and blew it away like a leaf torn from an oak, so that it fell a hundred and thirty yards off or more.

"I say, Quatermain," I said to him when the beaters were up, "do you often do this sort of thing?"

"Well," he answered, with a dry smile, "the last time I had to load three shots as quickly as that was at rather larger game. It was at elephants. I killed them all three as dead as I killed those woodcocks; but it very nearly went the other way, I can tell you; I mean that they very nearly killed me."

Just at that moment the keeper came up, "Did you happen to get one of them there cocks, sir?" he said, with the air of a man who did not in the least expect an answer in the affirmative.

"Well, yes, Jeffries," answered Quatermain; "you will find one of them by the hedge, and another about fifty yards out by the plough there to the left——"

The keeper had turned to go, looking a little astonished, when Quatermain called him back.

"Stop a bit, Jeffries," he said. "You see that pollard about one hundred and forty yards off? Well, there should be another woodcock down in a line with it, about sixty paces out in the field."

"Well, if that bean't the very smartest bit of shooting," murmured Jeffries, and departed.

After that we went home, and in due course Sir Henry Curtis and Captain Good arrived for dinner, the latter arrayed in the tightest and most ornamental dress-suit I ever saw. I remember that the waistcoat was adorned with five pink coral buttons.

It was a very pleasant dinner. Old Quatermain was in an excellent humour; induced, I think, by the recollection of his triumph over the doubting Jeffries. Good, too, was full of anecdotes. He told us a most miraculous story of how he once went shooting ibex in Kashmir. These ibex, according to Good, he stalked early and late for four entire days. At last on the morning of the fifth day he succeeded in getting within range of the flock, which consisted of a magnificent old ram with horns so long that I am afraid to mention their measure, and five or six females. Good crawled upon his stomach, painfully taking shelter behind rocks, till he was within two hundred yards; then he drew a fine bead upon the old ram. At this moment, however, a diversion occurred. Some wandering native of the hills appeared upon a distant mountain top. The females turned, and rushing over a rock vanished from Good's ken. But the old ram took a bolder course. In front of him stretched a mighty crevasse at least thirty feet in width. He went at it with a bound. Whilst he was in mid-air Good fired, and killed him dead. The ram turned a complete somersault in space, and fell in such fashion that his horns hooked themselves upon a big projection of the opposite cliffs. There he hung, till Good, after a long and painful détour, gracefully dropped a lasso over him and fished him up.

This moving tale of wild adventure was received with undeserved incredulity.

"Well," said Good, "if you fellows won't believe my story when I tell it—a perfectly true story mind—perhaps one of you will give us a better; I'm not particular if it is true or not." And he lapsed into a dignified silence.

"Now, Quatermain," I said, "don't let Good beat you, let us hear how you killed those elephants you were talking about this evening just after you shot the woodcocks."

"Well," said Quatermain, dryly, and with something like a twinkle in his brown eyes, "it is very hard fortune for a man to have to follow on Good's "spoor." Indeed if it were not for that running giraffe which, as you will remember, Curtis, we saw Good bowl over with a Martini rifle at three hundred yards, I should almost have said that this was an impossible tale."

Here Good looked up with an air of indignant innocence.

"However," he went on, rising and lighting his pipe, "if you fellows like, I will spin you a yarn. I was telling one of you the other night about those three lions and how the lioness finished my unfortunate 'voorlooper,' Jim-Jim, the boy whom we buried in the bread-bag.

"Well, after this little experience I thought that I would settle down a bit, so I entered upon a venture with a man who, being of a speculative mind, had conceived the idea of running a store at Pretoria upon strictly cash principles. The arrangement was that I should find the capital and he the experience. Our partnership was not of a long duration. The Boers refused to pay cash, and at the end of four months my partner had the capital and I had the experience. After this I came to the conclusion that store-keeping was not in my line, and having four hundred pounds left, I sent my boy Harry to a school in Natal, and buying an outfit with what remained of the money, started upon a big trip.

"This time I determined to go further afield than I had ever been before; so I took a passage for a few pounds in a trading brig that ran between Durban and Delagoa Bay. From Delagoa Bay I marched inland accompanied by twenty porters, with the idea of striking up north, towards the Limpopo, and keeping parallel to the coast, but at a distance of about one hundred and fifty miles from it. For the first twenty days of our journey we suffered a good deal from fever, that is, my men did, for I think that I am fever proof. Also I was hard put to it to keep the camp in meat, for although the country proved to be very sparsely populated, there was but little game about. Indeed, during all that time I hardly killed anything larger than a waterbuck, and, as you know, waterbuck's flesh is not very appetising food. On the twentieth day, however, we came to the banks of a largish river, the Gonooroo it was called. This I crossed, and then struck inland towards a great range of mountains, the blue crests of which we could see lying on the distant heavens like a shadow, a continuation, as I believe, of the Drakensberg range that skirts the coast of Natal. From this main range a great spur shoots out some fifty miles or so towards the coast, ending abruptly in one tremendous peak. This spur I discovered separated the territories of two chiefs named Nala and Wambe, Wambe's territory being to the north, and Nala's to the south. Nala ruled a tribe of bastard Zulus called the Butiana, and Wambe a much larger tribe, called the Matuku, which presents marked Bantu characteristics. For instance, they have doors and verandahs to their huts, work skins perfectly, and wear a waistcloth and not a moocha. At this time the Butiana were more or less subject to the Matuku, having been surprised by them some twenty years before and mercilessly slaughtered down. The tribe was now recovering itself, however, and as you may imagine, it did not love the Matuku.

"Well, I heard as I went along that elephants were very plentiful in the dense forests which lie upon the slopes and at the foot of the mountains that border Wambe's territory. Also I heard a very ill report of that worthy himself, who lived in a kraal upon the side of the mountain, which was so strongly fortified as to be practically impregnable. It was said that he was the most cruel chief in this part of Africa, and that he had murdered in cold blood an entire party of English gentlemen, who, some seven years before, had gone into his country to hunt elephants. They took an old friend of mine with them as guide, John Every by name, and often had I mourned over his untimely death. All the same, Wambe or no Wambe, I determined to hunt elephants in his country. I never was afraid of natives, and I was not going to show the white feather now. I am a bit of a fatalist, as you fellows know, so I came to the conclusion that if it was fated that Wambe should send me to join my old friend John Every, I should have to go, and there was an end of it. Meanwhile, I meant to hunt elephants with a peaceful heart.

"On the third day from the date of our sighting the great peak, we found ourselves beneath its shadow. Still following the course of the river which wound through the forests at the base of the peak, we entered the territory of the redoubtable Wambe. This, however, was not accomplished without a certain difference of opinion between my bearers and myself, for when we reached the spot where Wambe's boundary was supposed to run, the bearers sat down and emphatically refused to go a step further. I sat down too, and argued with them, putting my fatalistic views before them as well as I was able. But I could not persuade them to look at the matter in the same light. 'At present,' they said, 'their skins were whole; if they went into Wambe's country without his leave they would soon be like a water- eaten leaf. It was very well for me to say that this would be Fate. Fate no doubt might be walking about in Wambe's country, but while they stopped outside they would not meet him.'

"'Well,' I said to Gobo, my head man, 'and what do you mean to do?'

"'We mean to go back to the coast, Macumazahn,' he answered insolently.

"'Do you?' I replied, for my bile was stirred. 'At any rate, Mr. Gobo, you and one or two others will never get there; see here, my friend,' and I took a repeating rifle and sat myself comfortably down, resting my back against a tree—'I have just breakfasted, and I had as soon spend the day here as anywhere else. Now if you or any of those men walk one step back from here, and towards the coast, I shall fire at you; and you know that I don't miss.'

"The man fingered the spear he was carrying—luckily all my guns were stacked against the tree—and then turned as though to walk away, the others keeping their eyes fixed upon him all the while. I rose and covered him with the rifle, and though he kept up a brave appearance of unconcern, I saw that he was glancing nervously at me all the time. When he had gone about twenty yards I spoke very quietly—

"'Now, Gobo,' I said, 'come back, or I shall fire.'

"Of course this was taking a very high hand; I had no real right to kill Gobo or anybody else because they objected to run the risk of death by entering the territory of a hostile chief. But I felt that if I wished to keep up any authority it was absolutely necessary that I should push matters to the last extremity short of actually shooting him. So I sat there, looking fierce as a lion, and keeping the sight of my rifle in a dead line for Gobo's ribs. Then Gobo, feeling that the situation was getting strained, gave in.

"'Don't shoot, Boss,' he shouted, throwing up his hand, 'I will come with you.'

"'I thought you would,' I answered quietly; 'you see Fate walks about outside Wambe's country as well as in it.'

"After that I had no more trouble, for Gobo was the ringleader, and when he collapsed the others collapsed also. Harmony being thus restored, we crossed the line, and on the following morning I began shooting in good earnest.

A Morning's Sport

"Moving some five or six miles round the base of the great peak of which I have spoken, we came the same day to one of the fairest bits of African country that I have seen outside of Kukuanaland. At this spot the mountain spur that runs out at right angles to the great range, which stretches its cloud-clad length north and south as far as the eye can reach, sweeps inwards with a vast and splendid curve. This curve measures some five-and-thirty miles from point to point, and across its moon-like segment the river flashed, a silver line of light. On the further side of the river is a measureless sea of swelling ground, a natural park covered with great patches of bush— some of them being many square miles in extent. These are separated one from another by glades of grass land, broken here and there with clumps of timber trees; and in some instances by curious isolated koppies, and even by single crags of granite that start up into the air as though they were monuments carved by man, and not tombstones set by nature over the grave of ages gone. On the west this beautiful plain is bordered by the lonely mountain, from the edge of which it rolls down toward the fever coast; but how far it runs to the north I cannot say—eight days' journey, according to the natives, when it is lost in an untravelled morass.

"On the hither side of the river the scenery is different. Along the edge of its banks, where the land is flat, are green patches of swamp. Then comes a wide belt of beautiful grass land covered thickly with game, and sloping up very gently to the borders of the forest, which, beginning at about a thousand feet above the level of the plain, clothes the mountain-side almost to its crest. In this forest grow great trees, most of them of the yellow-wood species. Some of these trees are so lofty, that a bird in their top branches would be out of range of an ordinary shot gun. Another peculiar thing about them is, that they are for the most part covered with a dense growth of the Orchilla moss; and from this moss the natives manufacture a most excellent deep purple dye, with which they stain tanned hides and also cloth, when they happen to get any of the latter. I do not think that I ever saw anything more remarkable than the appearance of one of these mighty trees festooned from top to bottom with trailing wreaths of this sad-hued moss, in which the wind whispers gently as it stirs them. At a distance it looks like the gray locks of a Titan crowned with bright green leaves, and here and there starred with the rich bloom of orchids.

"The night of that day on which I had my little difference of opinion with Gobo, we camped by the edge of this great forest, and on the following morning at daylight I started out shooting. As we were short of meat I determined to kill a buffalo, of which there were plenty about, before looking for traces of elephants. Not more than half a mile from camp we came across a trail broad as a cart-road, evidently made by a great herd of buffaloes which had passed up at dawn from their feeding ground in the marshes, to spend the day in the cool air of the uplands. This trail I followed boldly; for such wind as there was blew straight down the mountain-side, that is, from the direction in which the buffaloes had gone, to me. About a mile further on the forest began to be dense, and the nature of the trail showed me that I must be close to my game. Another two hundred yards and the bush was so thick that, had it not been for the trail, we could scarcely have passed through it. As it was, Gobo, who carried my eight-bore rifle (for I had the .570-express in my hand), and the other two men whom I had taken with me, showed the very strongest dislike to going any further, pointing out that there was 'no room to run away.' I told them that they need not come unless they liked, but that I was certainly going on; and then, growing ashamed, they came.

"Another fifty yards, and the trail opened into a little glade. I knelt down and peeped and peered, but no buffalo could I see. Evidently the herd had broken up here—I knew that from the spoor—and penetrated the opposite bush in little troops. I crossed the glade, and choosing one line of spoor, followed it for some sixty yards, when it became clear to me that I was surrounded by buffaloes; and yet so dense was the cover that I could not see any. A few yards to my left I could hear one rubbing its horns against a tree, while from my right came an occasional low and throaty grunt which told me that I was uncomfortably near an old bull. I crept on towards him with my heart in my mouth, as gently as though I were walking upon eggs for a bet, lifting every little bit of wood in my path, and placing it behind me lest it should crack and warn the game. After me in single file came my three retainers, and I don't know which of them looked the most frightened. Presently Gobo touched my leg; I glanced round, and saw him pointing slantwise towards the left. I lifted my head a little and peeped over a mass of creepers; beyond the creepers was a dense bush of sharp-pointed aloes, of that kind of which the leaves project laterally, and on the other side of the aloes, not fifteen paces from us, I made out the horns, neck, and the ridge of the back of a tremendous old bull. I took my eight-bore, and getting on to my knee prepared to shoot him through the neck, taking my chance of cutting his spine. I had already covered him as well as the aloe leaves would allow, when he gave a kind of sigh and lay down.

"I looked round in dismay. What was to be done now? I could not see to shoot him lying down, even if my bullet would have pierced the intervening aloes—which was doubtful—and if I stood up he would either run away or charge me. I reflected, and came to the conclusion that the only thing to do was to lie down also; for I did not fancy wandering after other buffaloes in that dense bush. If a buffalo lies down, it is clear that he must get up again some time, so it was only a case of patience—'fighting the fight of sit down,' as the Zulus say.

"Accordingly I sat down and lighted a pipe, thinking that the smell of it might reach the buffalo and make him get up. But the wind was the wrong way, and it did not; so when it was done I lit another. Afterwards I had cause to regret that pipe.

"Well, we squatted like this for between half and three quarters of an hour, till at length I began to grow heartily sick of the performance. It was about as dull a business as the last hour of a comic opera. I could hear buffaloes snorting and moving all round, and see the red- beaked tic birds flying up off their backs, making a kind of hiss as they did so, something like that of the English missel-thrush, but I could not see a single buffalo. As for my old bull, I think he must have slept the sleep of the just, for he never even stirred.

"Just as I was making up my mind that something must be done to save the situation, my attention was attracted by a curious grinding noise. At first I thought that it must be a buffalo chewing the cud, but was obliged to abandon the idea because the noise was too loud. I shifted myself round and stared through the cracks in the bush, in the direction whence the sound seemed to come, and once I thought that I saw something gray moving about fifty yards off, but could not make certain. Although the grinding noise still continued I could see nothing more, so I gave up thinking about it, and once again turned my attention to the buffalo. Presently, however, something happened. Suddenly from about forty yards away there came a tremendous snorting sound, more like that made by an engine getting a heavy train under weigh than anything else in the world.

"'By Jove,' I thought, turning round in the direction from which the grinding sound had come, 'that must be a rhinoceros, and he has got our wind.' For, as you fellows know, there is no mistaking the sound made by a rhinoceros when he gets wind of you.

"Another second, and I heard a most tremendous crashing noise. Before I could think what to do, before I could even get up, the bush behind me seemed to burst asunder, and there appeared not eight yards from us, the great horn and wicked twinkling eye of a charging rhinoceros. He had winded us or my pipe, I do not know which, and, after the fashion of these brutes, had charged up the scent. I could not rise, I could not even get the gun up, I had no time. All that I was able to do was to roll over as far out of the monster's path as the bush would allow. Another second and he was over me, his great bulk towering above me like a mountain, and, upon my word, I could not get his smell out of my nostrils for a week. Circumstances impressed it on my memory, at least I suppose so. His hot breath blew upon my face, one of his front feet just missed my head, and his hind one actually trod upon the loose part of my trousers and pinched a little bit of my skin. I saw him pass over me lying as I was upon my back, and next second I saw something else. My men were a little behind me, and therefore straight in the path of the rhinoceros. One of them flung himself backwards into the bush, and thus avoided him. The second with a wild yell sprung to his feet, and bounded like an india-rubber ball right into the aloe bush, landing well among the spikes. But the third, it was my friend Gobo, could not by any means get away. He managed to gain his feet, and that was all. The rhinoceros was charging with his head low; his horn passed between Gobo's legs, and feeling something on his nose, he jerked it up. Away went Gobo, high into the air. He turned a complete somersault at the apex of the curve, and as he did so, I caught sight of his face. It was gray with terror, and his mouth was wide open. Down he came, right on to the great brute's back, and that broke his fall. Luckily for him the rhinoceros never turned, but crashed straight through the aloe bush, only missing the man who had jumped into it by about a yard.

"Then followed a complication. The sleeping buffalo on the further side of the bush, hearing the noise, sprang to his feet, and for a second, not knowing what to do, stood still. At that instant the huge rhinoceros blundered right on to him, and getting his horn beneath his stomach gave him such a fearful dig that the buffalo was turned over on to his back, while his assailant went a most amazing cropper over his carcase. In another moment, however, the rhinoceros was up, and wheeling round to the left, crashed through the bush down-hill and towards the open country.

"Instantly the whole place became alive with alarming sounds. In every direction troops of snorting buffaloes charged through the forest, wild with fright, while the injured bull on the further side of the bush began to bellow like a mad thing. I lay quite still for a moment, devoutly praying that none of the flying buffaloes would come my way. Then when the danger lessened I got on to my feet, shook myself, and looked round. One of my boys, he who had thrown himself backward into the bush, was already half way up a tree—if heaven had been at the top of it he could not have climbed quicker. Gobo was lying close to me, groaning vigorously, but, as I suspected, quite unhurt; while from the aloe bush into which No. 3 had bounded like a tennis ball, issued a succession of the most piercing yells.

"I looked, and saw that this unfortunate fellow was in a very tight place. A great spike of aloe had run through the back of his skin waist-belt, though without piercing his flesh, in such a fashion that it was impossible for him to move, while within six feet of him the injured buffalo bull, thinking, no doubt, that he was the aggressor, bellowed and ramped to get at him, tearing the thick aloes with his great horns. That no time was to be lost, if I wished to save the man's life, was very clear. So seizing my eight-bore, which was fortunately uninjured, I took a pace to the left, for the rhinoceros had enlarged the hole in the bush, and aimed at the point of the buffalo's shoulder, since on account of my position I could not get a fair side shot for the heart. As I did so I saw that the rhinoceros had given the bull a tremendous wound in the stomach, and that the shock of the encounter had put his left hind-leg out of joint at the hip. I fired, and the bullet striking the shoulder broke it, and knocked the buffalo down. I knew that he could not get up any more, because he was now injured fore and aft, so notwithstanding his terrific bellows I scrambled round to where he was. There he lay glaring furiously and tearing up the soil with his horns. Stepping up to within two yards of him I aimed at the vertebra of his neck and fired. The bullet struck true, and with a thud he dropped his head upon the ground, groaned, and died.

"This little matter having been attended to with the assistance of Gobo, who had now found his feet, I went on to extricate our unfortunate companion from the aloe bush. This we found a thorny task, but at last he was dragged forth uninjured, though in a very pious and prayerful frame of mind. His 'spirit had certainly looked that way,' he said, or he would now have been dead. As I never like to interfere with true piety, I did not venture to suggest that his spirit had deigned to make use of my eight-bore in his interest.

"Having despatched this boy back to the camp to tell the bearers to come and cut the buffalo up, I bethought me that I owed that rhinoceros a grudge which I should love to repay. So without saying a word of what was in my mind to Gobo, who was now more than ever convinced that Fate walked about loose in Wambe's country, I just followed on the brute's spoor. He had crashed through the bush till he reached the little glade. Then moderating his pace somewhat, he had followed the glade down its entire length, and once more turned to the right through the forest, shaping his course for the open land that lies between the edge of the bush and the river. Having followed him for a mile or so further, I found myself quite on the open. I took out my glasses and searched the plain. About a mile ahead was something brown—as I thought, the rhinoceros. I advanced another quarter of a mile, and looked once more —it was not the rhinoceros, but a big ant-heap. This was puzzling, but I did not like to give it up, because I knew from his spoor that he must be somewhere ahead. But as the wind was blowing straight from me towards the line that he had followed, and as a rhinoceros can smell you for about a mile, it would not, I felt, be safe to follow his trail any further; so I made a détour of a mile and more, till I was nearly opposite the ant-heap, and then once more searched the plain. It was no good, I could see nothing of him, and was about to give it up and start after some oryx I saw on the skyline, when suddenly at a distance of about three hundred yards from the ant-heap, and on its further side, I saw my rhino stand up in a patch of grass.

"'Heavens!' I thought to myself, 'he's off again;' but no, after standing staring for a minute or two he once more lay down.

"Now I found myself in a quandary. As you know, a rhinoceros is a very short-sighted brute, indeed his sight is as bad as his scent is good. Of this fact he is perfectly aware, but he always makes the most of his natural gifts. For instance, when he lies down he invariably does so with his head down wind. Thus, if any enemy crosses his wind he will still be able to escape, or attack him; and if, on the other hand, the danger approaches up wind he will at least have a chance of seeing it. Otherwise, by walking delicately, one might actually kick him up like a partridge, if only the advance was made up wind.

"Well, the point was, how on earth should I get within shot of this rhinoceros? After much deliberation I determined to try a side approach, thinking that in this way I might get a shoulder shot. Accordingly we started in a crouching attitude, I first, Gobo holding on to my coat tails, and the other boy on to Gobo's moocha. I always adopt this plan when stalking big game, for if you follow any other system the bearers will get out of line. We arrived within three hundred yards safely enough, and then the real difficulties began. The grass had been so closely eaten off by game that there was scarcely any cover. Consequently it was necessary to go on to our hands and knees, which in my case involved laying down the eight-bore at every step and then lifting it up again. However, I wriggled along somehow, and if it had not been for Gobo and his friend no doubt everything would have gone well. But as you have, I dare say, observed, a native out stalking is always of that mind which is supposed to actuate an ostrich—so long as his head is hidden he seems to think that nothing else can be seen. So it was in this instance, Gobo and the other boy crept along on their hands and toes with their heads well down, but, though unfortunately I did not notice it till too late, bearing the fundamental portions of their frames high in the air. Now all animals are quite as suspicious of this end of mankind as they are of his face, and of that fact I soon had a proof. Just when we had got within about two hundred yards, and I was congratulating myself that I had not had this long crawl with the sun beating on the back of my neck like a furnace for nothing, I heard the hissing note of the rhinoceros birds, and up flew four or five of them from the brute's back, where they had been comfortably employed in catching tics. Now this performance on the part of the birds is to a rhinoceros what the word 'cave' is to a schoolboy—it puts him on the *qui vive* at once. Before the birds were well in the air I saw the grass stir.

"'Down you go,' I whispered to the boys, and as I did so the rhinoceros got up and glared suspiciously around. But he could see nothing, indeed if we had been standing up I doubt if he would have seen us at that distance; so he merely gave two or three sniffs and then lay down, his head still down wind, the birds once more settling on his back.

"But it was clear to me that he was sleeping with one eye open, being generally in a suspicious and unchristian frame of mind, and that it was useless to proceed further on this stalk, so we quietly withdrew to consider the position and study the ground. The results were not satisfactory. There was absolutely no cover about except the ant-heap, which was some three hundred yards from the rhinoceros upon his up-wind side. I knew that if I tried to stalk him in front I should fail, and so I should if I attempted to do so from the further side—he or the birds would see me; so I came to a conclusion: I would go to the ant-heap, which would give him my wind, and instead of stalking him I would let him stalk me. It was a bold step, and one which I should never advise a hunter to take, but somehow I felt as though rhino and I must play the hand out.

"I explained my intentions to the men, who both held up their arms in horror. Their fears for my safety were a little mitigated, however, when I told them that I did not expect them to come with me.

"Gobo breathed a prayer that I might not meet Fate walking about, and the other one sincerely trusted that my spirit might look my way when the rhinoceros charged, and then they both departed to a place of safety.

"Taking my eight-bore, and half-a-dozen spare cartridges in my pocket, I made a détour, and reaching the ant-heap in safety lay down. For a moment the wind had dropped, but presently a gentle puff of air passed over me, and blew on towards the rhinoceros. By the way, I wonder what it is that smells so strong about a man? Is it his body or his breath? I have never been able to make out, but I saw it stated the other day, that in the duck decoys the man who is working the ducks holds a little piece of burning turf before his mouth, and that if he does this they cannot smell him, which looks as though it were the breath. Well, whatever it was about me that attracted his attention, the rhinoceros soon smelt me, for within half a minute after the puff of wind had passed me he was on his legs, and turning round to get his head up wind. There he stood for a few seconds and sniffed, and then he began to move, first of all at a trot, then, as the scent grew stronger, at a furious gallop. On he came, snorting like a runaway engine, with his tail stuck straight up in the air; if he had seen me lie down there he could not have made a better line. It was rather nervous work, I can tell you, lying there waiting for his onslaught, for he looked like a mountain of flesh. I determined, however, not to fire till I could plainly see his eye, for I think that rule always gives one the right distance for big game; so I rested my rifle on the ant-heap and waited for him, kneeling. At last, when he was about forty yards away, I saw that the time had come, and aiming straight for the middle of the chest I pulled.

"*Thud* went the heavy bullet, and with a tremendous snort over rolled the rhinoceros beneath its shock, just like a shot rabbit. But if I had thought that he was done for I was mistaken, for in another second he was up again, and coming at me as hard as ever, only with his head held low. I waited till he was within ten yards, in the hope that he would expose his chest, but he would do nothing of the sort; so I just had to fire at his head with the left barrel, and take my chance. Well, as luck would have it, of course the animal put its horn in the way of the bullet, which cut clean through it about three inches above the root and then glanced off into space.

"After that things got rather serious. My gun was empty and the rhinoceros was rapidly arriving, so rapidly indeed that I came to the conclusion that I had better make way for him. Accordingly I jumped to my feet and ran to the right as hard as I could go. As I did so he arrived full tilt, knocked my friendly ant-heap flat, and for the third time that day went a most magnificent cropper. This gave me a few seconds' start, and I ran down wind—my word, I did run! Unfortunately, however, my modest retreat was observed, and the rhinoceros, as soon as he had found his legs again, set to work to run after me. Now no man on earth can run so fast as an irritated rhinoceros can gallop, and I knew that he must soon catch me up. But having some slight experience of this sort of thing, luckily for myself, I kept my head, and as I fled I managed to open my rifle, get the old cartridges out, and put in two fresh ones. To do this I was obliged to steady my pace a little, and by the time that I had snapped the rifle to I heard the beast snorting and thundering away within a few paces of my back. I stopped, and as I did so rapidly cocked the rifle and slued round upon my heel. By this time the brute was within six or seven yards of me, but luckily his head was up. I lifted the rifle and fired at him. It was a snap shot, but the bullet struck him in the chest within three inches of the first, and found its way into his lungs. It did not stop him, however, so all I could do was to bound to one side, which I did with surprising activity, and as he brushed past me to fire the other barrel into his side. That did for him. The ball passed in behind the shoulder and right through his heart. He fell over on to his side, gave one more awful squeal—a dozen pigs could not have made such a noise—and promptly died, keeping his wicked eyes wide open all the time.

"As for me, I blew my nose, and going up to the rhinoceros sat on his head, and reflected that I had done a capital morning's shooting.

The First Round

"After this, as it was now midday, and I had killed enough meat, we marched back triumphantly to camp, where I proceeded to concoct a stew of buffalo beef and compressed vegetables. When this was ready we ate the stew, and then I took a nap. About four o'clock, however, Gobo woke me up, and told me that the head man of one of Wambe's kraals had arrived to see me. I ordered him to be brought up, and presently he came, a little, wizened, talkative old man, with a waistcloth round his middle, and a greasy, frayed kaross made of the skins of rock rabbits over his shoulders.

"I told him to sit down, and then abused him roundly. 'What did he mean,' I asked, 'by disturbing me in this rude way? How did he dare to cause a person of my quality and evident importance to be awakened in order to interview his entirely contemptible self?'

"I spoke thus because I knew that it would produce an impression on him. Nobody, except a really great man, he would argue, would dare to speak to him in that fashion. Most savages are desperate bullies at heart, and look on insolence as a sign of power.

"The old man instantly collapsed. He was utterly overcome, he said; his heart was split in two, and well realized the extent of his misbehaviour. But the occasion was very urgent. He heard that a mighty hunter was in the neighbourhood, a beautiful white man, how beautiful he could not have imagined had he not seen (this to me!), and he came to beg his assistance. The truth was, that three bull elephants such as no man ever saw had for years been the terror of their kraal, which was but a small place—a cattle kraal of the great chief Wambe's, where they lived to keep the cattle. And now of late these elephants had done them much damage; but last night they had destroyed a whole patch of mealie land, and he feared that if they came back they would all starve next season for want of food. Would the mighty white man then be pleased to come and kill the elephants? It would be easy for him to do—oh, most easy! It was only necessary that he should hide himself in a tree, for there was a full moon, and then when the elephants appeared he would speak to them with the gun, and they would fall down dead, and there would be an end of their troubling.

"Of course I hummed and hawed, and made a great favour of consenting to his proposal, though really I was delighted to have such a chance. One of the conditions that I made was that a messenger should at once be despatched to Wambe, whose kraal was two days' journey from where I was, telling him that I proposed to come and pay my respects to him in a few days, and to ask his formal permission to shoot in his country. Also I intimated that I was prepared to present him with 'hongo,' that is, blackmail, and that I hoped to do a little trade with him in ivory, of which I heard he had a great quantity.

"This message the old gentleman promised to despatch at once, though there was something about his manner which showed me that he was doubtful as to how it would be received. After that we struck our camp and moved on to the kraal, which we reached about an hour before sunset. This kraal was a collection of huts surrounded by a slight thorn-fence, perhaps there were ten of them in all. It was situated in a kloof of the mountain down which a rivulet flowed. The kloof was densely wooded, but for some distance above the kraal it was free from bush, and here on the rich deep ground brought down by the rivulet were the cultivated lands, in extent somewhere about twenty or twenty-five acres. On the kraal side of these lands stood a single hut, that served for a mealie store, which at the moment was used as a dwelling-place by an old woman, the first wife of our friend the head man.

"It appears that this lady, having had some difference of opinion with her husband about the extent of authority allowed to a younger and more amiable wife, had refused to dwell in the kraal any more, and, by way of marking her displeasure, had taken up her abode among the mealies. As the issue will show, she was, it happened, cutting off her nose to spite her face.

"Close by this hut grew a large baobab tree. A glance at the mealie grounds showed me that the old head man had not exaggerated the mischief done by the elephants to his crops, which were now getting ripe. Nearly half of the entire patch was destroyed. The great brutes had eaten all they could, and the rest they had trampled down. I went up to their spoor and started back in amazement—never had I seen such a spoor before. It was simply enormous, more especially that of one old bull, that carried, so said the natives, but a single tusk. One might have used any of the footprints for a hip-bath.

"Having taken stock of the position, my next step was to make arrangements for the fray. The three bulls, according to the natives, had been spoored into the dense patch of bush above the kloof. Now it seemed to me very probable that they would return to-night to feed on the remainder of the ripening mealies. If so, there was a bright moon, and it struck me that by the exercise of a little ingenuity I might bag one or more of them without exposing myself to any risk, which, having the highest respect for the aggressive powers of bull elephants, was a great consideration to me.

"This then was my plan. To the right of the huts as you look up the kloof, and commanding the mealie lands, stands the baobab tree that I have mentioned. Into that baobab tree I made up my mind to go. Then if the elephants appeared I should get a shot at them. I announced my intentions to the head man of the kraal, who was delighted. 'Now,' he said, 'his people might sleep in peace, for while the mighty white hunter sat aloft like a spirit watching over the welfare of his kraal what was there to fear?'

"I told him that he was an ungrateful brute to think of sleeping in peace while, perched like a wounded vulture on a tree, I watched for his welfare in wakeful sorrow; and once more he collapsed, and owned that my words were 'sharp but just.'

"However, as I have said, confidence was completely restored; and that evening everybody in the kraal, including the superannuated victim of jealousy in the little hut where the mealie cobs were stored, went to bed with a sense of sweet security from elephants and all other animals that prowl by night.

"For my part, I pitched my camp below the kraal; and then, having procured a beam of wood from the head man—rather a rotten one, by the way—I set it across two boughs that ran out laterally from the baobab tree, at a height of about twenty-five feet from the ground, in such fashion that I and another man could sit upon it with our legs hanging down, and rest our backs against the bole of the tree. This done I went back to the camp and ate my supper. About nine o'clock, half-an- hour before the moon-rise, I summoned Gobo, who, thinking that he had seen about enough of the delights of big game hunting for that day, did not altogether relish the job; and, despite his remonstrances, gave him my eight-bore to carry, I having the .570-express. Then we set out for the tree. It was very dark, but we found it without difficulty, though climbing it was a more complicated matter. However, at last we got up and sat down, like two little boys on a form that is too high for them, and waited. I did not dare to smoke, because I remembered the rhinoceros, and feared that the elephants might wind the tobacco if they should come my way, and this made the business more wearisome, so I fell to thinking and wondering at the completeness of the silence.

"At last the moon came up, and with it a moaning wind, at the breath of which the silence began to whisper mysteriously. Lonely enough in the newborn light looked the wide expanse of mountain, plain, and forest, more like some vision of a dream, some reflection from a fair world of peace beyond our ken, than the mere face of garish earth made soft with sleep. Indeed, had it not been for the fact that I was beginning to find the log on which I sat very hard, I should have grown quite sentimental over the beautiful sight; but I will defy anybody to become sentimental when seated in the damp, on a very rough beam of wood, and half-way up a tree. So I merely made a mental note that it was a particularly lovely night, and turned my attention to the prospect of elephants. But no elephants came, and after waiting for another hour or so, I think that what between weariness and disgust, I must have dropped into a gentle doze. Presently I awoke with a start. Gobo, who was perched close to me, but as far off as the beam would allow—for neither white man nor black like the aroma which each vows is the peculiar and disagreeable property of the other—was faintly, very faintly clicking his forefinger against his thumb. I knew by this signal, a very favourite one among native hunters and gun-bearers, that he must have seen or heard something. I looked at his face, and saw that he was staring excitedly towards the dim edge of the bush beyond the deep green line of mealies. I stared too, and listened. Presently I heard a soft large sound as though a giant were gently stretching out his hands and pressing back the ears of standing corn. Then came a pause, and then, out into the open majestically stalked the largest elephant I ever saw or ever shall see. Heavens! what a monster he was; and how the moonlight gleamed upon his one splendid tusk—for the other was missing—as he stood among the mealies gently moving his enormous ears to and fro, and testing the wind with his trunk. While I was still marvelling at his girth, and speculating upon the weight of that huge tusk, which I swore should be my tusk before very long, out stepped a second bull and stood beside him. He was not quite so tall, but he seemed to me to be almost thicker-set than the first; and even in that light I could see that both his tusks were perfect. Another pause, and the third emerged. He was shorter than either of the others, but higher in the shoulder than No. 2; and when I tell you, as I afterwards learnt from actual measurement, that the smallest of these mighty bulls measured twelve feet one and a half inches at the shoulder, it will give you some idea of their size. The three formed into line and stood still for a minute, the one-tusked bull gently caressing the elephant on the left with his trunk.

"Then they began to feed, walking forward and slightly to the right as they gathered great bunches of the sweet mealies and thrust them into their mouths. All this time they were more than a hundred and twenty yards away from me (this I knew, because I had paced the distances from the tree to various points), much too far to allow of my attempting a shot at them in that uncertain light. They fed in a semicircle, gradually drawing round towards the hut near my tree, in which the corn was stored and the old woman slept.

"This went on for between an hour and an hour and a half, till, what between excitement and hope, that maketh the heart sick, I grew so weary that I was actually contemplating a descent from the tree and a moonlight stalk. Such an act in ground so open would have been that of a stark staring lunatic, and that I should even have been contemplating it will show you the condition of my mind. But everything comes to him who knows how to wait, and sometimes too to him who doesn't, and so at last those elephants, or rather one of them, came to me.

"After they had fed their fill, which was a very large one, the noble three stood once more in line some seventy yards to the left of the hut, and on the edge of the cultivated lands, or in all about eighty- five yards from where I was perched. Then at last the one with a single tusk made a peculiar rattling noise in his trunk, just as though he were blowing his nose, and without more ado began to walk deliberately toward the hut where the old woman slept. I made my rifle ready and glanced up at the moon, only to discover that a new complication was looming in the immediate future. I have said that a wind rose with the moon. Well, the wind brought rain-clouds along its track. Several light ones had already lessened the light for a little while, though without obscuring it, and now two more were coming up rapidly, both of them very black and dense. The first cloud was small and long, and the one behind big and broad. I remember noticing that the pair of them bore a most comical resemblance to a dray drawn by a very long raw-boned horse. As luck would have it, just as the elephant arrived within twenty-five yards or so of me, the head of the horse- cloud floated over the face of the moon, rendering it impossible for me to fire. In the faint twilight which remained, however, I could just make out the gray mass of the great brute still advancing towards the hut. Then the light went altogether and I had to trust to my ears. I heard him fumbling with his trunk, apparently at the roof of the hut; next came a sound as of straw being drawn out, and then for a little while there was complete silence.

"The cloud began to pass; I could see the outline of the elephant; he was standing with his head quite over the top of the hut. But I could not see his trunk, and no wonder, for it was *inside the hut.* He had thrust it through the roof, and, attracted no doubt by the smell of the mealies, was groping about with it inside. It was growing light now, and I got my rifle ready, when suddenly there was a most awful yell, and I saw the trunk reappear, and in its mighty fold the old woman who had been sleeping in the hut. Out she came through the hole like a periwinkle on the point of a pin, still wrapped up in her blanket, and with her skinny arms and legs stretched to the four points of the compass, and as she did so, gave that most alarming screech. I really don't know who was the most frightened, she, or I, or the elephant. At any rate the last was considerably startled; he had been fishing for mealies—the old woman was a mere accident, and one that greatly discomposed his nerves. He gave a sort of trumpet, and threw her away from him right into the crown of a low mimosa tree, where she stuck shrieking like a metropolitan engine. The old bull lifted his tail, and flapping his great ears prepared for flight. I put up my eight-bore, and aiming hastily at the point of his shoulder (for he was broadside on), I fired. The report rang out like thunder, making a thousand echoes in the quiet hills. I saw him go down all of a heap as though he were stone dead. Then, alas! whether it was the kick of the heavy rifle, or the excited bump of that idiot Gobo, or both together, or merely an unhappy coincidence, I do not know, but the rotten beam broke and I went down too, landing flat at the foot of the tree upon a certain humble portion of the human frame. The shock was so severe that I felt as though all my teeth were flying through the roof of my mouth, but although I sat slightly stunned for a few seconds, luckily for me I fell light, and was not in any way injured.

"Meanwhile the elephant began to scream with fear and fury, and, attracted by his cries, the other two charged up. I felt for my rifle; it was not there. Then I remembered that I had rested it on a fork of the bough in order to fire, and doubtless there it remained. My position was now very unpleasant. I did not dare to try and climb the tree again, which, shaken as I was, would have been a task of some difficulty, because the elephants would certainly see me, and Gobo, who had clung to a bough, was still aloft with the other rifle. I could not run because there was no shelter near. Under these circumstances I did the only thing feasible, clambered round the trunk as softly as possible, and keeping one eye on the elephants, whispered to Gobo to bring down the rifle, and awaited the development of the situation. I knew that if the elephants did not see me—which, luckily, they were too enraged to do—they would not smell me, for I was up-wind. Gobo, however, either did not, or, preferring the safety of the tree, would not hear me. He said the former, but I believed the latter, for I knew that he was not enough of a sportsman to really enjoy shooting elephants by moonlight in the open. So there I was behind my tree, dismayed, unarmed, but highly interested, for I was witnessing a remarkable performance.

"When the two other bulls arrived the wounded elephant on the ground ceased to scream, but began to make a low moaning noise, and to gently touch the wound near his shoulder, from which the blood was literally spouting. The other two seemed to understand; at any rate, they did this. Kneeling down on either side, they placed their trunks and tusks underneath him, and, aided by his own efforts, with one great lift got him on to his feet. Then leaning against him on either side to support him, they marched off at a walk in the direction of the village. It was a pitiful sight, and even then it made me feel a brute.

"Presently, from a walk, as the wounded elephant gathered himself together a little, they broke into a trot, and after that I could follow them no longer with my eyes, for the second black cloud came up over the moon and put her out, as an extinguisher puts out a dip. I say with my eyes, but my ears gave me a very fair notion of what was going on. When the cloud came up the three terrified animals were heading directly for the kraal, probably because the way was open and the path easy. I fancy that they grew confused in the darkness, for when they came to the kraal fence they did not turn aside, but crashed straight through it. Then there were 'times,' as the Irish servant- girl says in the American book. Having taken the fence, they thought that they might as well take the kraal also, so they just ran over it. One hive-shaped hut was turned quite over on to its top, and when I arrived upon the scene the people who had been sleeping there were bumbling about inside like bees disturbed at night, while two more were crushed flat, and a third had all its side torn out. Oddly enough, however, nobody was hurt, though several people had a narrow escape of being trodden to death.

"On arrival I found the old head man in a state painfully like that favoured by Greek art, dancing about in front of his ruined abodes as vigorously as though he had just been stung by a scorpion.

"I asked him what ailed him, and he burst out into a flood of abuse. He called me a Wizard, a Sham, a Fraud, a Bringer of bad luck! I had promised to kill the elephants, and I had so arranged things that the elephants had nearly killed him, etc.

"This, still smarting, or rather aching, as I was from that most terrific bump, was too much for my feelings, so I just made a rush at my friend, and getting him by the ear, I banged his head against the doorway of his own hut, which was all that was left of it.

"'You wicked old scoundrel,' I said, 'you dare to complain about your own trifling inconveniences, when you gave me a rotten beam to sit on, and thereby delivered me to the fury of the elephant' (*bump! bump! bump!*), 'when your own wife' (*bump!*) 'has just been dragged out of her hut' (*bump!*) 'like a snail from its shell, and thrown by the Earth-shaker into a tree' (*bump! bump!*).

"'Mercy, my father, mercy!' gasped the old fellow. 'Truly I have done amiss—my heart tells me so.'

"'I should hope it did, you old villain' (*bump!*).

"'Mercy, great white man! I thought the log was sound. But what says the unequalled chief—is the old woman, my wife, indeed dead? Ah, if she is dead all may yet prove to have been for the very best;' and he clasped his hands and looked up piously to heaven, in which the moon was once more shining brightly.

"I let go his ear and burst out laughing, the whole scene and his devout aspirations for the decease of the partner of his joys, or rather woes, were so intensely ridiculous.

"'No, you old iniquity,' I answered; 'I left her in the top of a thorn-tree, screaming like a thousand bluejays. The elephant put her there.'

"'Alas! alas!' he said, 'surely the back of the ox is shaped to the burden. Doubtless, my father, she will come down when she is tired;' and without troubling himself further about the matter, he began to blow at the smouldering embers of the fire.

"And, as a matter of fact, she did appear a few minutes later, considerably scratched and startled, but none the worse.

"After that I made my way to my little camp, which, fortunately, the elephants had not walked over, and wrapping myself up in a blanket, was soon fast asleep.

"And so ended my first round with those three elephants.

The Last Round

"On the morrow I woke up full of painful recollections, and not without a certain feeling of gratitude to the Powers above that I was there to wake up. Yesterday had been a tempestuous day; indeed, what between buffalo, rhinoceros, and elephant, it had been very tempestuous. Having realized this fact, I next bethought me of those magnificent tusks, and instantly, early as it was, broke the tenth commandment. I coveted my neighbours tusks, if an elephant could be said to be my neighbour *de jure*, as certainly, so recently as the previous night, he had been *de facto*—a much closer neighbour than I cared for, indeed. Now when you covet your neighbour's goods, the best thing, if not the most moral thing, to do is to enter his house as a strong man armed, and take them. I was not a strong man, but having recovered my eight-bore I was armed, and so was the other strong man— the elephant with the tusks. Consequently I prepared for a struggle to the death. In other words, I summoned my faithful retainers, and told them that I was now going to follow those elephants to the edge of the world, if necessary. They showed a certain bashfulness about the business, but they did not gainsay me, because they dared not. Ever since I had prepared with all due solemnity to execute the rebellious Gobo they had conceived a great respect for me.

"So I went up to bid adieu to the old head man, whom I found alternately contemplating the ruins of his kraal and, with the able assistance of his last wife, thrashing the jealous lady who had slept in the mealie hut, because she was, as he declared, the fount of all his sorrows.

"Leaving them to work a way through their domestic differences, I levied a supply of vegetable food from the kraal in consideration of services rendered, and left them with my blessing. I do not know how they settled matters, because I have not seen them since.

"Then I started on the spoor of the three bulls. For a couple of miles or so below the kraal—as far, indeed, as the belt of swamp that borders the river—the ground is at this spot rather stony, and clothed with scattered bushes. Rain had fallen towards the daybreak, and this fact, together with the nature of the soil, made spooring a very difficult business. The wounded bull had indeed bled freely, but the rain had washed the blood off the leaves and grass, and the ground being so rough and hard did not take the footmarks so clearly as was convenient. However, we got along, though slowly, partly by the spoor, and partly by carefully lifting leaves and blades of grass, and finding blood underneath them, for the blood gushing from a wounded animal often falls upon their inner surfaces, and then, of course, unless the rain is very heavy, it is not washed away. It took us something over an hour and a half to reach the edge of the marsh, but once there our task became much easier, for the soft soil showed plentiful evidences of the great brutes' passage. Threading our way through the swampy land, we came at last to a ford of the river, and here we could see where the poor wounded animal had lain down in the mud and water in the hope of easing himself of his pain, and could see also how his two faithful companions had assisted him to rise again. We crossed the ford, and took up the spoor on the further side, and followed it into the marsh-like land beyond. No rain had fallen on this side of the river, and the blood-marks were consequently much more frequent.

"All that day we followed the three bulls, now across open plains, and now through patches of bush. They seemed to have travelled on almost without stopping, and I noticed that as they went the wounded bull recovered his strength a little. This I could see from his spoor, which had become firmer, and also from the fact that the other two had ceased to support him. At last evening closed in, and having travelled some eighteen miles, we camped, thoroughly tired out.

"Before dawn on the following day we were up, and the first break of light found us once more on the spoor. About half-past five o'clock we reached the place where the elephants had fed and slept. The two unwounded bulls had taken their fill, as the condition of the neighbouring bushes showed, but the wounded one had eaten nothing. He had spent the night leaning against a good-sized tree, which his weight had pushed out of the perpendicular. They had not long left this place, and could not be very far ahead, especially as the wounded bull was now again so stiff after his night's rest that for the first few miles the other two had been obliged to support him. But elephants go very quick, even when they seem to be travelling slowly, for shrub and creepers that almost stop a man's progress are no hindrance to them. The three had now turned to the left, and were travelling back again in a semicircular line toward the mountains, probably with the idea of working round to their old feeding grounds on the further side of the river.

"There was nothing for it but to follow their lead, and accordingly we followed with industry. Through all that long hot day did we tramp, passing quantities of every sort of game, and even coming across the spoor of other elephants. But, in spite of my men's entreaties, I would not turn aside after these. I would have those mighty tusks or none.

"By evening we were quite close to our game, probably within a quarter of a mile, but the bush was dense, and we could see nothing of them, so once more we must camp, thoroughly disgusted with our luck. That night, just after the moon rose, while I was sitting smoking my pipe with my back against a tree, I heard an elephant trumpet, as though something had startled it, and not three hundred yards away. I was very tired, but my curiosity overcame my weariness, so, without saying a word to any of the men, all of whom were asleep, I took my eight- bore and a few spare cartridges, and steered toward the sound. The game path which we had been following all day ran straight on in the direction from which the elephant had trumpeted. It was narrow, but well trodden, and the light struck down upon it in a straight white line. I crept along it cautiously for some two hundred yards, when it opened suddenly into a most beautiful glade some hundred yards or more in width, wherein tall grass grew and flat-topped trees stood singly. With the caution born of long experience I watched for a few moments before I entered the glade, and then I saw why the elephant had trumpeted. There in the middle of the glade stood a large maned lion. He stood quite still, making a soft purring noise, and waving his tail to and fro. Presently the grass about forty yards on the hither side of him gave a wide ripple, and a lioness sprang out of it like a flash, and bounded noiselessly up to the lion. Reaching him, the great cat halted suddenly, and rubbed her head against his shoulder. Then they both began to purr loudly, so loudly that I believe that in the stillness one might have heard them two hundred yards or more away.

"After a time, while I was still hesitating what to do, either they got a whiff of my wind, or they wearied of standing still, and determined to start in search of game. At any rate, as though moved by a common impulse, they bounded suddenly away, leap by leap, and vanished in the depths of the forest to the left. I waited for a little while longer to see if there were any more yellow skins about, and seeing none, came to the conclusion that the lions must have frightened the elephants away, and that I had taken my stroll for nothing. But just as I was turning back I thought that I heard a bough break upon the further side of the glade, and, rash as the act was, I followed the sound. I crossed the glade as silently as my own shadow. On its further side the path went on. Albeit with many fears, I went on too. The jungle growth was so thick here that it almost met overhead, leaving so small a passage for the light that I could scarcely see to grope my way along. Presently, however, it widened, and then opened into a second glade slightly smaller than the first, and there, on the further side of it, about eighty yards from me, stood the three enormous elephants.

"They stood thus:—Immediately opposite and facing me was the wounded one-tusked bull. He was leaning his bulk against a dead thorn-tree, the only one in the place, and looked very sick indeed. Near him stood the second bull as though keeping a watch over him. The third elephant was a good deal nearer to me and broadside on. While I was still staring at them, this elephant suddenly walked off and vanished down a path in the bush to the right.

"There are now two things to be done—either I could go back to the camp and advance upon the elephants at dawn, or I could attack them at once. The first was, of course, by far the wiser and safer course. To engage one elephant by moonlight and single-handed is a sufficiently rash proceeding; to tackle three was little short of lunacy. But, on the other hand, I knew that they would be on the march again before daylight, and there might come another day of weary trudging before I could catch them up, or they might escape me altogether.

"'No,' I thought to myself, 'faint heart never won fair tusk. I'll risk it, and have a slap at them. But how?' I could not advance across the open, for they would see me; clearly the only thing to do was to creep round in the shadow of the bush and try to come upon them so. So I started. Seven or eight minutes of careful stalking brought me to the mouth of the path down which the third elephant had walked. The other two were now about fifty yards from me, and the nature of the wall of bush was such that I could not see how to get nearer to them without being discovered. I hesitated, and peeped down the path which the elephant had followed. About five yards in, it took a turn round a shrub. I thought that I would just have a look behind it, and advanced, expecting that I should be able to catch a sight of the elephant's tail. As it happened, however, I met his trunk coming round the corner. It is very disconcerting to see an elephant's trunk when you expect to see his tail, and for a moment I stood paralyzed almost under the vast brute's head, for he was not five yards from me. He too halted, threw up his trunk and trumpeted preparatory to a charge. I was in for it now, for I could not escape either to the right or left, on account of the bush, and I did not dare turn my back. So I did the only thing that I could do—raised the rifle and fired at the black mass of his chest. It was too dark for me to pick a shot; I could only brown him, as it were.

"The shot rung out like thunder on the quiet air, and the elephant answered it with a scream, then dropped his trunk and stood for a second or two as still as though he had been cut in stone. I confess that I lost my head; I ought to have fired my second barrel, but I did not. Instead of doing so, I rapidly opened my rifle, pulled out the old cartridge from the right barrel and replaced it. But before I could snap the breech to, the bull was at me. I saw his great trunk fly up like a brown beam, and I waited no longer. Turning, I fled for dear life, and after me thundered the elephant. Right into the open glade I ran, and then, thank Heaven, just as he was coming up with me the bullet took effect on him. He had been shot right through the heart, or lungs, and down he fell with a crash, stone dead.

"But in escaping from Scylla I had run into the jaws of Charybdis. I heard the elephant fall, and glanced round. Straight in front of me, and not fifteen paces away, were the other two bulls. They were staring about, and at that moment they caught sight of me. Then they came, the pair of them—came like thunderbolts, and from different angles. I had only time to snap my rifle to, lift it, and fire, almost at haphazard, at the head of the nearest, the unwounded bull.

"Now, as you know, in the case of the African elephant, whose skull is convex, and not concave like that of the Indian, this is always a most risky and very frequently a perfectly useless shot. The bullet loses itself in the masses of bone, that is all. But there is one little vital place, and should the bullet happen to strike there, it will follow the channel of the nostrils—at least I suppose it is that of the nostrils—and reach the brain. And this was what happened in the present case—the ball struck the fatal spot in the region of the eye and travelled to the brain. Down came the great bull all of a heap, and rolled on to his side as dead as a stone. I swung round at that instant to face the third, the monster bull with one tusk that I had wounded two days before. He was already almost over me, and in the dim moonlight seemed to tower above me like a house. I lifted the rifle and pulled at his neck. It would not go off! Then, in a flash, as it were, I remembered that it was on the half-cock. The lock of this barrel was a little weak, and a few days before, in firing at a cow eland, the left barrel had jarred off at the shock of the discharge of the right, knocking me backwards with the recoil; so after that I had kept it on the half-cock till I actually wanted to fire it.

"I gave one desperate bound to the right, and, my lame leg notwithstanding, I believe that few men could have made a better jump. At any rate, it was none too soon, for as I jumped I felt the wind made by the tremendous downward stroke of the monster's trunk. Then I ran for it.

"I ran like a buck, still keeping hold of my gun, however. My idea, so far as I could be said to have any fixed idea, was to bolt down the pathway up which I had come, like a rabbit down a burrow, trusting that he would lose sight of me in the uncertain light. I sped across the glade. Fortunately the bull, being wounded, could not go full speed; but wounded or no, he could go quite as fast as I could. I was unable to gain an inch, and away we went, with just about three feet between our separate extremities. We were at the other side now, and a glance served to show me that I had miscalculated and overshot the opening. To reach it now was hopeless; I should have blundered straight into the elephant. So I did the only thing I could do: I swerved like a course hare, and started off round the edge of the glade, seeking for some opening into which I could plunge. This gave me a moment's start, for the bull could not turn as quickly as I could, and I made the most of it. But no opening could I see; the bush was like a wall. We were speeding round the edge of the glade, and the elephant was coming up again. Now he was within about six feet, and now, as he trumpeted or rather screamed, I could feel the fierce hot blast of his breath strike upon my head. Heavens! how it frightened me!

"We were three parts round the glade now, and about fifty yards ahead was the single large dead thorn-tree against which the bull had been leaning. I spurted for it; it was my last chance of safety. But spurt as I would, it seemed hours before I got there. Putting out my right hand, I swung round the tree, thus bringing myself face to face with the elephant. I had not time to lift the rifle to fire, I had barely time to cock it, and run sideways and backward, when he was on to me. Crash! he came, striking the tree full with his forehead. It snapped like a carrot about forty inches from the ground. Fortunately I was clear of the trunk, but one of the dead branches struck me on the chest as it went down and swept me to the ground. I fell upon my back, and the elephant blundered past me as I lay. More by instinct than anything else I lifted the rifle with one hand and pulled the trigger. It exploded, and, as I discovered afterwards, the bullet struck him in the ribs. But the recoil of the heavy rifle held thus was very severe; it bent my arm up, and sent the butt with a thud against the top of my shoulder and the side of my neck, for the moment quite paralyzing me, and causing the weapon to jump from my grasp. Meanwhile the bull was rushing on. He travelled for some twenty paces, and then suddenly he stopped. Faintly I reflected that he was coming back to finish me, but even the prospect of imminent and dreadful death could not rouse me into action. I was utterly spent; I could not move.

"Idly, almost indifferently, I watched his movements. For a moment he stood still, next he trumpeted till the welkin rang, and then very slowly, and with great dignity, he knelt down. At this point I swooned away.

"When I came to myself again I saw from the moon that I must have been insensible for quite two hours. I was drenched with dew, and shivering all over. At first I could not think where I was, when, on lifting my head, I saw the outline of the one-tusked bull still kneeling some five-and-twenty paces from me. Then I remembered. Slowly I raised myself, and was instantly taken with a violent sickness, the result of over-exertion, after which I very nearly fainted a second time. Presently I grew better, and considered the position. Two of the elephants were, as I knew, dead; but how about No. 3? There he knelt in majesty in the lonely moonlight. The question was, was he resting, or dead? I rose on my hands and knees, loaded my rifle, and painfully crept a few paces nearer. I could see his eye now, for the moonlight fell full upon it—it was open, and rather prominent. I crouched and watched; the eyelid did not move, nor did the great brown body, or the trunk, or the ear, or the tail—nothing moved. Then I knew that he must be dead.

"I crept up to him, still keeping the rifle well forward, and gave him a thump, reflecting as I did so how very near I had been to being thumped instead of thumping. He never stirred; certainly he was dead, though to this day I do not know if it was my random shot that killed him, or if he died from concussion of the brain consequent upon the tremendous shock of his contact with the tree. Anyhow, there he was. Cold and beautiful he lay, or rather knelt, as the poet nearly puts it. Indeed, I do not think that I have ever seen a sight more imposing in its way than that of the mighty beast crouched in majestic death, and shone upon by the lonely moon.

"While I stood admiring the scene, and heartily congratulating myself upon my escape, once more I began to feel sick. Accordingly, without waiting to examine the other two bulls, I staggered back to the camp, which in due course I reached in safety. Everybody in it was asleep. I did not wake them, but having swallowed a mouthful of brandy I threw off my coat and shoes, rolled myself up in a blanket, and was soon fast asleep.

"When I woke it was already light, and at first I thought that, like Joseph, I had dreamed a dream. At that moment, however, I turned my head, and quickly knew that it was no dream, for my neck and face were so stiff from the blow of the butt-end of the rifle that it was agony to move them. I collapsed for a minute or two. Gobo and another man, wrapped up like a couple of monks in their blankets, thinking that I was still asleep, were crouched over a little fire they had made, for the morning was damp and chilly, and holding sweet converse.

"Gobo said that he was getting tired of running after elephants which they never caught. Macumazahn (that is, myself) was without doubt a man of parts, and of some skill in shooting, but also he was a fool. None but a fool would run so fast and far after elephants which it was impossible to catch, when they kept cutting the spoor of fresh ones. He certainly was a fool, but he must not be allowed to continue in his folly; and he, Gobo, had determined to put a stop to it. He should refuse to accompany him any further on so mad a hunt.

"'Yes,' the other answered, 'the poor man certainly was sick in his head, and it was quite time that they checked his folly while they still had a patch of skin left upon their feet. Moreover, he for his part certainly did not like this country of Wambe's, which really was full of ghosts. Only the last night he had heard the spooks at work— they were out shooting, at least it sounded as though they were. It was very queer, but perhaps their lunatic of a master——'

"'Gobo, you scoundrel!' I shouted out at this juncture, sitting bolt upright on the blankets, 'stop idling there and make me some coffee.'

"Up sprang Gobo and his friend, and in half a moment were respectfully skipping about in a manner that contrasted well with the lordly contempt of their previous conversation. But all the time they were in earnest in what they said about hunting the elephants any further, for before I had finished my coffee they came to me in a body, and said that if I wanted to follow those elephants I must follow them myself, for they would not go.

"I argued with them, and affected to be much put out. The elephants were close at hand, I said; I was sure of it; I had heard them trumpet in the night.

"'Yes,' answered the men mysteriously, 'they too had heard things in the night, things not nice to hear; they had heard the spooks out shooting, and no longer would they remain in a country so vilely haunted.'

"'It was nonsense,' I replied. 'If ghosts went out shooting, surely they would use air-guns and not black powder, and one would not hear an air-gun. Well, if they were cowards, and would not come, of course I could not force them to, but I would make a bargain with them. They should follow those elephants for one half-hour more, then if we failed to come upon them I would abandon the pursuit, and we would go straight to Wambe, chief of the Matuku, and give him hongo.'

"To this compromise the men agreed readily. Accordingly about half-an- hour later we struck our camp and started, and notwithstanding my aches and bruises, I do not think that I ever felt in better spirits in my life. It is something to wake up in the morning and remember that in the dead of the night, single-handed, one has given battle to and overthrown three of the largest elephants in Africa, slaying them with three bullets. Such a feat to my knowledge had never been done before, and on that particular morning I felt a very 'tall man of my hands' indeed. The only thing I feared was, that should I ever come to tell the story nobody would believe it, for when a strange tale is told by a hunter, people are apt to think it is necessarily a lie, instead of being only probably so.

"Well, we passed on till, having crossed the first glade where I had seen the lions, we reached the neck of bush that separated it from the second glade, where the dead elephants were. And here I began to take elaborate precautions, amongst others ordering Gobo to keep some yards ahead and look out sharp, as I thought that the elephants might be about. He obeyed my instructions with a superior smile, and pushed ahead. Presently I saw him pull up as though he had been shot, and begin to snap his fingers faintly.

"'What is it?' I whispered.

"'The elephant, the great elephant with one tusk kneeling down.'

"I crept up beside him. There knelt the bull as I had left him last night, and there too lay the other bulls.

"'Do these elephants sleep?' I whispered to the astonished Gobo.

"'Yes, Macumazahn, they sleep.'

"'Nay, Gobo, they are dead.'

"'Dead? How can they be dead? Who killed them?'

"'What do people call me, Gobo?'

"'They call you Macumazahn.'

"'And what does Macumazahn mean?'

"'It means the man who keeps his eyes open, the man who gets up in the night.'

"'Yes, Gobo, and I am that man. Look, you idle, lazy cowards; while you slept last night I rose, and alone I hunted those great elephants, and slew them by the moonlight. To each of them I gave one bullet and only one, and it fell dead. Look,' and I advanced into the glade, 'here is my spoor, and here is the spoor of the great bull charging after me, and there is the tree that I took refuge behind; see, the elephant shattered it in his charge. Oh, you cowards, you who would give up the chase while the blood spoor steamed beneath your nostrils, see what I did single-handed while you slept, and be ashamed.'

"'*Ou!*' said the men, '*Ou!* Koos! Koos y umcool!' (Chief, great Chief!) And then they held their tongues, and going up to the three dead beasts, gazed upon them in silence.

"But after that those men looked upon me with awe as being almost more than mortal. No mere man, they said, could have slain those three elephants alone in the night-time. I never had any further trouble with them. I believe that if I had told them to jump over a precipice and that they would take no harm, they would have believed me.

"Well, I went up and examined the bulls. Such tusks as they had I never saw and never shall see again. It took us all day to cut them out; and when they reached Delagoa Bay, as they did ultimately, though not in my keeping, the single tusk of the big bull scaled one hundred and sixty pounds, and the four other tusks averaged ninety-nine and a half pounds—a most wonderful, indeed an almost unprecedented, lot of ivory. Unfortunately I was forced to saw the big tusk in two, otherwise we could not have carried it."

"Oh, Quatermain, you barbarian!" I broke in here, "the idea of spoiling such a tusk! Why, I would have kept it whole if I had been obliged to drag it myself."

"Oh yes, young man," he answered, "it is all very well for you to talk like that, but if you had found yourself in the position which it was my privilege to occupy a few hours afterwards, it is my belief that you would have thrown the tusks away altogether and taken to your heels."

"Oh," said Good, "so that isn't the end of the yarn? A very good yarn, Quatermain, by the way—I couldn't have made up a better one myself."

The old gentleman looked at Good severely, for it irritated him to be chaffed about his stories.

"I don't know what you mean, Good. I don't see that there is any comparison between a true story of adventure and the preposterous tales which you invent about ibex hanging by their horns. No, it is not the end of the story; the most exciting part is to come. But I have talked enough for to-night; and if you go on in that way, Good, it will be some time before I begin again."

"Sorry I spoke, I'm sure," said Good, humbly. "Let's have a split to show that there is no ill-feeling." And they did.

The Message of Maiwa

On the following evening we once more dined together, and Quatermain, after some pressure, was persuaded to continue his story—for Good's remark still rankled in his breast.

"At last," he went on, "a few minutes before sunset, the task was finished. We had laboured at it all day, stopping only once for dinner, for it is no easy matter to hew out five such tusks as those which now lay before me in a white and gleaming line. It was a dinner worth eating, too, I can tell you, for we dined off the heart of the great one-tusked bull, which was so big that the man whom I sent inside the elephant to look for his heart was forced to remove it in two pieces. We cut it into slices and fried it with fat, and I never tasted heart to equal it, for the meat seemed to melt in one's mouth. By the way, I examined the jaw of the elephant; it never grew but one tusk; the other had not been broken off, nor was it present in a rudimentary form.

"Well, there lay the five beauties, or rather four of them, for Gobo and another man were engaged in sawing the grand one in two. At last with many sighs I ordered them to do this, but not until by practical experiment I had proved that it was impossible to carry it in any other way. One hundred and sixty pounds of solid ivory, or rather more in its green state, is too great a weight for two men to bear for long across a broken country. I sat watching the job and smoking the pipe of contentment, when suddenly the bush opened, and a very handsome and dignified native girl, apparently about twenty years of age, stood before me, carrying a basket of green mealies upon her head.

"Although I was rather surprised to see a native girl in such a wild spot, and, so far as I knew, a long way from any kraal, the matter did not attract my particular notice; I merely called to one of the men, and told him to bargain with the woman for the mealies, and ask her if there were any more to be bought in the neighbourhood. Then I turned my head and continued to superintend the cutting of the tusk. Presently a shadow fell upon me. I looked up, and saw that the girl was standing before me, the basket of mealies still on her head.

"'Marême, Marême,' she said, gently clapping her hands together. The word Marême among these Matuku (though she was no Matuku) answers to the Zulu 'Koos,' and the clapping of hands is a form of salutation very common among the tribes of the Basutu race.

"'What is it, girl?' I asked her in Sisutu. 'Are those mealies for sale?'

"'No, great white hunter,' she answered in Zulu, 'I bring them as a gift.'

"'Good,' I replied; 'set them down.'

"'A gift for a gift, white man.'

"'Ah,' I grumbled, 'the old story—nothing for nothing in this wicked world. What do you want—beads?'

"She nodded, and I was about to tell one of the men to go and fetch some from one of the packs, when she checked me.

"'A gift from the giver's own hand is twice a gift,' she said, and I thought that she spoke meaningly.

"'You mean that you want me to give them to you myself?'

"'Surely.'

"I rose to go with her. 'How is it that, being of the Matuku, you speak in the Zulu tongue?' I asked suspiciously.

"'I am not of the Matuku,' she answered as soon as we were out of hearing of the men. 'I am of the people of Nala, whose tribe is the Butiana tribe, and who lives there,' and she pointed over the mountain. 'Also I am one of the wives of Wambe,' and her eyes flashed as she said the name.

"'And how did you come here?'

"'On my feet,' she answered laconically.

"We reached the packs, and undoing one of them, I extracted a handful of beads. 'Now,' I said, 'a gift for a gift. Hand over the mealies.'

"She took the beads without even looking at them, which struck me as curious, and setting the basket of mealies on the ground, emptied it.

"At the bottom of the basket were some curiously-shaped green leaves, rather like the leaves of the gutta-percha tree in shape, only somewhat thicker and of a more fleshy substance. As though by hazard, the girl picked one of these leaves out of the basket and smelt it. Then she handed it to me. I took the leaf, and supposing that she wished me to smell it also, was about to oblige her by doing so, when my eye fell upon some curious red scratches on the green surface of the leaf.

"'Ah,' said the girl (whose name, by the way, was Maiwa), speaking beneath her breath, 'read the signs, white man.'

"Without answering her I continued to stare at the leaf. It had been scratched or rather written upon with a sharp tool, such as a nail, and wherever this instrument had touched it, the acid juice oozing through the outer skin had turned a rusty blood colour. Presently I found the beginning of the scrawl, and read this in English, and covering the surface of the leaf and of two others that were in the basket.

"'I hear that a white man is hunting in the Matuku country. This is to warn him to fly over the mountain to Nala. Wambe sends an impi at daybreak to eat him up, because he has hunted before bringing hongo. For God's sake, whoever you are, try to help me. I have been the slave of this devil Wambe for nearly seven years, and am beaten and tortured continually. He murdered all the rest of us, but kept me because I could work iron. Maiwa, his wife, takes this; she is flying to Nala her father because Wambe killed her child. Try to get Nala to attack Wambe; Maiwa can guide them over the mountain. You won't come for nothing, for the stockade of Wambe's private kraal is made of elephants' tusks. For God's sake, don't desert me, or I shall kill myself. I can bear this no longer.

"'John Every.'

"'Great heavens!' I gasped. 'Every!—why, it must be my old friend.' The girl, or rather the woman Maiwa, pointed to the other side of the leaf, where there was more writing. It ran thus—'I have just heard that the white man is called Macumazahn. If so, it must be my friend Quatermain. Pray Heaven it is, for I know he won't desert an old chum in such a fix as I am. It isn't that I'm afraid of dying, I don't care if I die, but I want to get a chance at Wambe first.'

"'No, old boy,' thought I to myself, 'it isn't likely that I am going to leave you there while there is a chance of getting you out. I have played fox before now—there's still a double or two left in me. I must make a plan, that's all. And then there's that stockade of tusks. I am not going to leave that either.' Then I spoke to the woman.

"'You are called Maiwa?'

"'It is so.'

"'You are the daughter of Nala and the wife of Wambe?'

"'It is so.'

"'You fly from Wambe to Nala?'

"'I do.'

"'Why do you fly? Stay, I would give an order,'—and calling to Gobo, I ordered him to get the men ready for instant departure. The woman, who, as I have said, was quite young and very handsome, put her hand into a little pouch made of antelope hide which she wore fastened round the waist, and to my horror drew from it the withered hand of a child, which evidently had been carefully dried in the smoke.

"'I fly for this cause,' she answered, holding the poor little hand towards me. 'See now, I bore a child. Wambe was its father, and for eighteen months the child lived and I loved it. But Wambe loves not his children; he kills them all. He fears lest they should grow up to slay one so wicked, and he would have killed this child also, but I begged its life. One day, some soldiers passing the hut saw the child and saluted him, calling him the "chief who soon shall be." Wambe heard, and was mad. He smote the babe, and it wept. Then he said that it should weep for good cause. Among the things that he had stolen from the white men whom he slew is a trap that will hold lions. So strong is the trap that four men must stand on it, two on either side, before it can be opened.'"

Here old Quatermain broke off suddenly.

"Look here, you fellows," he said, "I can't bear to go on with this part of the story, because I never could stand either seeing or talking of the sufferings of children. You can guess what that devil did, and what the poor mother was forced to witness. Would you believe it, she told me the tale without a tremor, in the most matter-of-fact way. Only I noticed that her eyelid quivered all the time.

"'Well,' I said, as unconcernedly as though I had been talking of the death of a lamb, though inwardly I was sick with horror and boiling with rage, 'and what do you mean to do about the matter, Maiwa, wife of Wambe?'

"'I mean to do this, white man,' she answered, drawing herself up to her full height, and speaking in tones as hard as steel and cold as ice—'I mean to work, and work, and work, to bring this to pass, and to bring that to pass, until at length it comes to pass that with these living eyes I behold Wambe dying the death that he gave to his child and my child.'

"'Well said,' I answered.

"'Ay, well said, Macumazahn, well said, and not easily forgotten. Who could forget, oh, who could forget? See where this dead hand rests against my side; so once it rested when alive. And now, though it is dead, now every night it creeps from its nest and strokes my hair and clasps my fingers in its tiny palm. Every night it does this, fearing lest I should forget. Oh, my child! my child! ten days ago I held thee to my breast, and now this alone remains of thee,' and she kissed the dead hand and shivered, but never a tear did she weep.

"'See now,' she went on, 'the white man, the prisoner at Wambe's kraal, he was kind to me. He loved the child that is dead, yes, he wept when its father slew it, and at the risk of his life told Wambe, my husband—ah, yes, my husband!—that which he is! He too it was who made a plan. He said to me, "Go, Maiwa, after the custom of thy people, go purify thyself in the bush alone, having touched a dead one. Say to Wambe thou goest to purify thyself alone for fifteen days, according to the custom of thy people. Then fly to thy father, Nala, and stir him up to war against Wambe for the sake of the child that is dead." This then he said, and his words seemed good to me, and that same night ere I left to purify myself came news that a white man hunted in the country, and Wambe, being mad with drink, grew very wrath, and gave orders that an impi should be gathered to slay the white man and his people and seize his goods. Then did the "Smiter of Iron" (Every) write the message on the green leaves, and bid me seek thee out, and show forth the matter, that thou mightest save thyself by flight; and behold, this thing have I done, Macumazahn, the hunter, the Slayer of Elephants.'

"'Ah,' I said, 'I thank you. And how many men be there in the impi of Wambe?'

"'A hundred of men and half a hundred.'

"'And where is the impi?'

"'There to the north. It follows on thy spoor. I saw it pass yesterday, but myself I guessed that thou wouldst be nigher to the mountain, and came this way, and found thee. To-morrow at the daybreak the slayers will be here.'

"'Very possibly,' I thought to myself; 'but they won't find Macumazahn. I have half a mind to put some strychnine into the carcases of those elephants for their especial benefit though.' I knew that they would stop to eat the elephants, as indeed they did, to our great gain, but I abandoned the idea of poisoning them, because I was rather short of strychnine."

"Or because you did not like to play the trick, Quatermain?" I suggested with a laugh.

"I said because I had not enough strychnine. It would take a great deal of strychnine to poison three elephants effectually," answered the old gentleman testily.

I said nothing further, but I smiled, knowing that old Allan could never have resorted to such an artifice, however severe his strait. But that was his way; he always made himself out to be a most unmerciful person.

"Well," he went on, "at that moment Gobo came up and announced that we were ready to march. 'I am glad that you are ready,' I said, 'because if you don't march, and march quick, you will never march again, that is all. Wambe has an impi out to kill us, and it will be here presently.'

"Gobo turned positively green, and his knees knocked together. 'Ah, what did I say?' he exclaimed. 'Fate walks about loose in Wambe's country.'

"'Very good; now all you have to do is to walk a little quicker than he does. No, no, you don't leave those elephant tusks behind—I am not going to part with them I can tell you.'

"Gobo said no more, but hastily directed the men to take up their loads, and then asked which way we were to run.

"'Ah,' I said to Maiwa, 'which way?'

"'There,' she answered, pointing towards the great mountain spur which towered up into the sky some forty miles away, separating the territories of Nala and Wambe—'there, below that small peak, is one place where men may pass, and one only. Also it can easily be blocked from above. If men pass not there, then they must go round the great peak of the mountain, two days' journey and half a day.'

"'And how far is the peak from us?'

"'All to-night shall you walk and all to-morrow, and if you walk fast, at sunset you shall stand on the peak.'

"I whistled, for that meant a five-and-forty miles trudge without sleep. Then I called to the men to take each of them as much cooked elephant's meat as he could carry conveniently. I did the same myself, and forced the woman Maiwa to eat some as we went. This I did with difficulty, for at that time she seemed neither to sleep nor eat nor rest, so fiercely was she set on vengeance.

"Then we started, Maiwa guiding us. After going for a half-hour over gradually rising ground, we found ourselves on the further edge of a great bush-clad depression something like the bottom of a lake. This depression, through which we had been travelling, was covered with bush to a very great extent, indeed almost altogether so, except where it was pitted with glades such as that wherein I had shot the elephants.

"At the top of this slope Maiwa halted, and putting her hand over her eyes looked back. Presently she touched me on the arm and pointed across the sea of forest towards a comparatively vacant space of country some six or seven miles away. I looked, and suddenly I saw something flash in the red rays of the setting sun. A pause, and then another quick flash.

"'What is it?' I asked.

"'It is the spears of Wambe's impi, and they travel fast,' she answered coolly.

"I suppose that my face showed how little I liked the news, for she went on—

"'Fear not; they will stay to feast upon the elephants, and while they feast we shall journey. We may yet escape.'

"After that we turned and pushed on again, till at length it grew so dark that we had to wait for the rising of the moon, which lost us time, though it gave us rest. Fortunately none of the men had seen that ominous flashing of the spears; if they had, I doubt if even I could have kept control of them. As it was, they travelled faster than I had ever known loaded natives to go before, so thorough-paced was their desire to see the last of Wambe's country. I, however, took the precaution to march last of all, fearing lest they should throw away their loads to lighten themselves, or, worse still, the tusks; for these kind of fellows would be capable of throwing anything away if their own skins were at stake. If the pious Æneas, whose story you were reading to me the other night, had been a mongrel Delagoa Bay native, Anchises would have had a poor chance of getting out of Troy, that is, if he was known to have made a satisfactory will.

"At moonrise we set out again, and with short occasional halts travelled till dawn, when we were forced to rest and eat. Starting once more, about half-past five, we crossed the river at noon. Then began the long toilsome ascent through thick bush, the same in which I shot the bull buffalo, only some twenty miles to the west of that spot, and not more than twenty-five miles on the hither side of Wambe's kraal. There were six or seven miles of this dense bush, and hard work it was to get through it. Next came a belt of scattered forest which was easier to pass, though, in revenge, the ground was steeper. This was about two miles wide, and we passed it by about four in the afternoon. Above this scattered bush lay a long steep slope of boulder-strewn ground, which ran up to the foot of the little peak some three miles away. As we emerged, footsore and weary, on to this inhospitable plain, some of the men looking round caught sight of the spears of Wambe's impi advancing rapidly not more than a mile behind us.

"At first there was a panic, and the bearers tried to throw off their loads and run, but I harangued them, calling out to them that certainly I would shoot the first man who did so and that if they would but trust in me I would bring them through the mess. Now, ever since I had killed those three elephants single-handed, I had gained great influence over these men, and they listened to me. So off we went as hard as ever we could go—the members of the Alpine Club would not have been in it with us. We made the boulders burn, as a Frenchman would say.

"When we had done about a mile the spears began to emerge from the belt of scattered bush, and the whoop of their bearers as they viewed us broke upon our ears. Quick as our pace had been before, it grew much quicker now, for terror lent wings to my gallant crew. But they were sorely tired, and the loads were heavy, so that run, or rather climb, as we would, Wambe's soldiers, a scrubby-looking lot of men armed with big spears and small shields, but without plumes, climbed considerably faster. The last mile of that pleasing chase was like a fox hunt, we being the fox, and always in view. What astonished me was the extraordinary endurance and activity shown by Maiwa. She never even flagged. I think that girl's muscles must have been made of iron, or perhaps it was the strength of her will that supported her. At any rate she reached the foot of the peak second, poor Gobo, who was an excellent hand at running away, being first.

"Presently I came up panting, and glanced at the ascent. Before us was a wall of rock about one hundred and fifty feet in height, upon which the strata were laid so as to form a series of projections sufficiently resembling steps to make the ascent easy, comparatively speaking, except at one spot, where it was necessary to climb over a projecting angle of cliff and bear a little to the left. It was not a really difficult place, but what made it awkward was, that immediately beneath this projection gaped a deep fissure or donga, on the brink of which we now stood, originally dug out, no doubt, by the rush of water from the peak and cliff. This gulf beneath would be trying to the nerves of a weak-headed climber at the critical point, and so it proved in the result. The projecting angle once passed, the remainder of the ascent was very simple. At the summit, however, the brow of the cliff hung over and was pierced by a single narrow path cut through it by water, in such fashion that a single boulder rolled into it at the top would make the cliff quite impassable to men without ropes.

"At this moment Wambe's soldiers were about a thousand yards from us, so it was evident that we had no time to lose. I at once ordered the men to commence the ascent, the girl Maiwa, who was familiar with the pass, going first to show them the way. Accordingly they began to mount with alacrity, pushing and lifting their loads in front of them. When the first of them, led by Maiwa, reached the projecting angle, they put down their loads upon a ledge of rock and clambered over. Once there, by lying on their stomachs upon a boulder, they could reach the loads which were held to them by the men beneath, and in this way drag them over the awkward place, whence they were carried easily to the top.

"But all of this took time, and meanwhile the soldiers were coming up fast, screaming and brandishing their big spears. They were now within about four hundred yards, and several loads, together with all the tusks, had yet to be got over the rock. I was still standing at the bottom of the cliff, shouting directions to the men above, but it occurred to me that it would soon be time to move. Before doing so, however, I thought that it might be well to try and produce a moral effect upon the advancing enemy. In my hand I held a Winchester repeating carbine, but the distance was too great for me to use it with effect, so I turned to Gobo, who was shivering with terror at my side, and handing him the carbine, took my express from him.

"The enemy was now about three hundred and fifty yards away, and the express was only sighted to three hundred. Still I knew that it could be trusted for the extra fifty yards. Running in front of Wambe's soldiers were two men—captains, I suppose—one of them very tall. I put up the three hundred yard flap, and sitting down with my back against the rock, I drew a long breath to steady myself, and covered the tall man, giving him a full sight. Feeling that I was on him, I pulled, and before the sound of the striking bullet could reach my ears, I saw the man throw up his arms and pitch forward on to his head. His companion stopped dead, giving me a fair chance. I rapidly covered him, and fired the left barrel. He turned round once, and then sank down in a heap. This caused the enemy to hesitate—they had never seen men killed at such a distance before, and thought that there was something uncanny about the performance. Taking advantage of the lull, I gave the express back to Gobo, and slinging the Winchester repeater over my back I began to climb the cliff.

"When we reached the projecting angle all the loads were over, but the tusks still had to be passed up, and owing to their weight and the smoothness of their surface, this was a very difficult task. Of course I ought to have abandoned the tusks; often and often have I since reproached myself for not doing so. Indeed, I think that my obstinacy about them was downright sinful, but I was always obstinate about such things, and I could not bear the idea of leaving those splendid tusks which had cost me so much pains and danger to come by. Well, it nearly cost me my life also, and did cost poor Gobo his, as will be seen shortly, to say nothing of the loss inflicted by my rifle on the enemy. When I reached the projection I found that the men, with their usual stupidity, were trying to hand up the tusks point first. Now the result of this was that those above had nothing to grip except the round polished surface of the ivory, and in the position in which they were, this did not give them sufficient hold to enable them to lift the weight. I told them to reverse the tusks and push them up, so that the rough and hollow ends came to the hands of the men above. This they did, and the first two were dragged up in safety.

"At this point, looking behind me, I saw the Matukus streaming up the slope in a rough extended order, and not more than a hundred yards away. Cocking the Winchester I turned and opened fire on them. I don't quite know how many I missed, but I do know that I never shot better in my life. I had to keep shifting myself from one enemy to the other, firing almost without getting a sight, that is, by the eye alone, after the fashion of the experts who break glass balls. But quick as the work was, men fell thick, and by the time that I had emptied the carbine of its twelve cartridges, for the moment the advance was checked. I rapidly pushed in some more cartridges, and hardly had I done so when the enemy, seeing that we were about to escape them altogether, came on once more with a tremendous yell. By this time the two halves of the single tusk of the great bull alone remained to be passed up. I fired and fired as effectively as before, but notwithstanding all that I could do, some men escaped my hail of bullets and began to ascend the cliff. Presently my rifle was again empty. I slung it over my back, and, drawing my revolver, turned to run for it, the attackers being now quite close. As I did so, a spear struck the cliff close to my head.

"The last half of the tusk was now vanishing over the rock, and I sung out to Gobo and the other man who had been pushing it up to vanish after it. Gobo, poor fellow, required no second invitation; indeed, his haste was his undoing. He went at the projecting rock with a bound. The end of the tusk was still hanging over, and instead of grasping the rock he caught at it. It twisted in his hand—he slipped —he fell; with one wild shriek he vanished into the abyss beneath, his falling body brushing me as it passed. For a moment we stood aghast, and presently the dull thud of his fall smote heavily upon our ears. Poor fellow, he had met the Fate which, as he declared, walked about loose in Wambe's country. Then with an oath the remaining man sprung at the rock and clambered over it in safety. Aghast at the awfulness of what had happened, I stood still, till I saw the great blade of a Matuku spear pass up between my feet. That brought me to my senses, and I began to clamber up the rock like a cat. I was half way round it. Already I had clasped the hand of that brave girl Maiwa, who came down to help me, the men having scrambled forward with the ivory, when I felt some one seize my ankle.

"'Pull, Maiwa, pull,' I gasped, and she certainly did pull. Maiwa was a very muscular woman, and never before did I appreciate the advantages of the physical development of females so keenly. She tugged at my left arm, the savage below tugged at my right leg, till I began to realize that something must give way ere long. Luckily I retained my presence of mind, like the man who threw his mother-in-law out of the window, and carried the mattress down-stairs, when a fire broke out in his house. My right hand was still free, and in it I held my revolver, which was secured to my wrist by a leather thong. The pistol was cocked, and I simply pointed it downwards and fired. The result was instantaneous—and so far as I am concerned, most satisfactory. The bullet hit the man beneath me somewhere, I am sure I don't know where; at any rate, he let go of my leg and plunged headlong into the gulf beneath to join Gobo. In another moment I was on the top of the rock, and going up the remaining steps like a lamplighter. A single other soldier appeared in pursuit, but one of my boys at the top fired my elephant gun at him. I don't know if he hit him or only frightened him; at any rate, he vanished whence he came. I do know, however, that he very nearly hit *me*, for I felt the wind of the bullet.

"Another thirty seconds, and I and the woman Maiwa were at the top of the cliff panting, but safe.

"My men, being directed thereto by Maiwa, had most fortunately rolled up some big boulders which lay about, and with these we soon managed to block the passage through the overhanging ridge of rock in such fashion that the soldiers below could not possibly climb over it. Indeed, so far as I could see, they did not even try to do so—their heart was turned to fat, as the Zulus say.

"Then having rested a few moments we took up the loads, including the tusks of ivory that had cost us so dear, and in silence marched on for a couple of miles or more, till we reached a patch of dense bush. And here, being utterly exhausted, we camped for the night, taking the precaution, however, of setting a guard to watch against any attempt at surprise.

The Plan of Campaign

"Notwithstanding all that we had gone through, perhaps indeed on account of it, for I was thoroughly worn out, I slept that night as soundly as poor Gobo, round whose crushed body the hyænas would now be prowling. Rising refreshed at dawn we went on our way towards Nala's kraal, which we reached at nightfall. It is built on open ground after the Zulu fashion, in a ring fence and with beehive huts. The cattle kraal is behind and a little to the left. Indeed, both from their habits and their talk it was easy to see that these Butiana belong to that section of the Bantu people which, since T'Chaka's time, has been known as the Zulu race. We did not see the chief Nala that night. His daughter Maiwa went on to his private huts as soon as we arrived, and very shortly afterwards one of his head men came to us bringing a sheep and some mealies and milk with him. 'The chief sent us greeting,' he said, 'and would see us on the morrow.' Meanwhile he was ordered to bring us to a place of resting, where we and our goods should be safe and undisturbed. Accordingly he led the way to some very good huts just outside Nala's private enclosure, and here we slept comfortably.

"On the morrow about eight o'clock the head man came again, and said that Nala requested that I would visit him. I followed him into the private enclosure and was introduced to the chief, a fine-looking man of about fifty, with very delicately-shaped hands and feet, and a rather nervous mouth. The chief was seated on a tanned ox-hide outside his hut. By his side stood his daughter Maiwa, and squatted on their haunches round him were some twenty head men or Indunas, whose number was continually added to by fresh arrivals. These men saluted me as I entered, and the chief rose and took my hand, ordering a stool to be brought for me to sit on. When this was done, with much eloquence and native courtesy he thanked me for protecting his daughter in the painful and dangerous circumstances in which she found herself placed, and also complimented me very highly upon what he was pleased to call the bravery with which I had defended the pass in the rocks. I answered in appropriate terms, saying that it was to Maiwa herself that thanks were due, for had it not been for her warning and knowledge of the country we should not have been here to-day; while as to the defence of the pass, I was fighting for my life, and that put heart into me.

"These courtesies concluded, Nala called upon his daughter Maiwa to tell her tale to the head men, and this she did most simply and effectively. She reminded them that she had gone as an unwilling bride to Wambe—that no cattle had been paid for her, because Wambe had threatened war if she was not sent as a free gift. Since she had entered the kraal of Wambe her days had been days of heaviness and her nights nights of weeping. She had been beaten, she had been neglected and made to do the work of a low-born wife—she, a chief's daughter. She had borne a child, and this was the story of the child. Then amidst a dead silence she told them the awful tale which she had already narrated to me. When she had finished, her hearers gave a loud ejaculation. '*Ou!*' they said, '*Ou!* Maiwa, daughter of Nala!'

"'Ay,' she went on with flashing eyes, 'ay, it is true; my mouth is as full of truth as a flower of honey, and for tears my eyes are like the dew upon the grass at dawn. It is true I saw the child die—here is the proof of it, councillors,' and she drew forth the little dead hand and held it before them.

"'*Ou!*' they said again, '*Ou!* it is the dead hand!'

"'Yes,' she continued, 'it is the dead hand of my dead child, and I bear it with me that I may never forget, never for one short hour, that I live that I may see Wambe die, and be avenged. Will you bear it, my father, that your daughter and your daughter's child should be so treated by a Matuku? Will ye bear it, men of my own people?'

"'No,' said an old Induna, rising, 'it is not to be borne. Enough have we suffered at the hands of these Matuku dogs and their loud-tongued chief; let us put it to the issue.'

"'It is not to be borne indeed,' said Nala; 'but how can we make head against so great a people?'

"'Ask of him—ask of Macumazahn, the wise white man,' said Maiwa, pointing at me.

"'How can we overcome Wambe, Macumazahn the hunter?'

"'How does the jackal overreach the lion, Nala?'

"'By cleverness, Macumazahn.'

"'So shall you overcome Wambe, Nala.'

"At this moment an interruption occurred. A man entered and said that messengers had arrived from Wambe.

"'What is their message?' asked Nala.

"'They come to ask that thy daughter Maiwa be sent back, and with her the white hunter.'

"'How shall I make answer to this, Macumazahn?' said Nala, when the man had withdrawn.

"'Thus shalt thou answer,' I said after reflection; 'say that the woman shall be sent and I with her, and then bid the messengers be gone. Stay, I will hide myself here in the hut that the men may not see me,' and I did.

"Shortly afterwards, through a crack in the hut, I saw the messengers arrive, and they were great truculent-looking fellows. There were four of them, and evidently they had travelled night and day. They entered with a swagger and squatted down before Nala.

"'Your business?' said Nala, frowning.

"'We come from Wambe, bearing the orders of Wambe to Nala his servant,' answered the spokesman of the party.

"'Speak,' said Nala, with a curious twitch of his nervous-looking mouth.

"'These are the words of Wambe: "Send back the woman, my wife, who has run away from my kraal, and send with her the white man who has dared to hunt in my country without my leave, and to slay my soldiers." These are the words of Wambe.'

"'And if I say I will not send them?' asked Nala.

"'Then on behalf of Wambe we declare war upon you. Wambe will eat you up. He will wipe you out; your kraals shall be stamped flat—so,' and with an expressive gesture he drew his hand across his mouth to show how complete would be the annihilation of that chief who dared to defy Wambe.

"'These are heavy words,' said Nala. 'Let me take counsel before I answer.'

"Then followed a little piece of acting that was really very creditable to the untutored savage mind. The heralds withdrew, but not out of sight, and Nala went through the show of earnestly consulting his Indunas. The girl Maiwa too flung herself at his feet, and appeared to weep and implore his protection, while he wrung his hands as though in doubt and tribulation of mind. At length he summoned the messengers to draw near, and addressed them, while Maiwa sobbed very realistically at his side.

"'Wambe is a great chief,' said Nala, 'and this woman is his wife, whom he has a right to claim. She must return to him, but her feet are sore with walking, she cannot come now. In eight days from this day she shall be delivered at the kraal of Wambe; I will send her with a party of my men. As for the white hunter and his men, I have nought to do with them, and cannot answer for their misdeeds. They have wandered hither unbidden by me, and I will deliver them back whence they came, that Wambe may judge them according to his law; they shall be sent with the girl. For you, go your ways. Food shall be given you without the kraal, and a present for Wambe in atonement of the ill-doing of my daughter. I have spoken.'

"At first the heralds seemed inclined to insist upon Maiwa's accompanying them then and there, but on being shown the swollen condition of her feet, ultimately they gave up the point and departed.

"When they were well out of the way I emerged from the hut, and we went on to discuss the situation and make our plans. First of all, as I was careful to explain to Nala, I was not going to give him my experience and services for nothing. I heard that Wambe had a stockade round his kraal made of elephant tusks. These tusks, in the event of our succeeding in the enterprise, I should claim as my perquisite, with the proviso that Nala should furnish me with men to carry them down to the coast.

"To this modest request Nala and the head men gave an unqualified and hearty assent, the more hearty perhaps because they never expected to get the ivory.

"The next thing I stipulated was, that if we conquered, the white man John Every should be handed over to me, together with any goods which he might claim. His cruel captivity was, I need hardly say, the only reason that induced me to join in so hair-brained an expedition, but I was careful from motives of policy to keep this fact in the background. Nala accepted this condition. My third stipulation was that no women or children should be killed. This being also agreed to, we went on to consider ways and means. Wambe, it appeared, was a very powerful petty chief, that is, he could put at least six thousand fighting men into the field, and always had from three to four thousand collected about his kraal, which was supposed to be impregnable. Nala, on the contrary, at such short notice could not collect more than from twelve to thirteen hundred men, though, being of the Zulu stock, they were of much better stuff for fighting purposes than Wambe's Matukus.

"These odds, though large, under the circumstances were not overwhelming. The real obstacle to our chance of success was the difficulty of delivering a crushing assault against Wambe's strong place. This was, it appeared, fortified all round with schanses or stone walls, and contained numerous caves and koppies in the hill-side and at the foot of the mountain which no force had ever been able to capture. It is said that in the time of the Zulu monarch Dingaan, a great impi of that king's having penetrated to this district, had delivered an assault upon the kraal then owned by a forefather of Wambe's, and been beaten back with the loss of more than a thousand men.

"Having thought the question over, I interrogated Maiwa closely as to the fortifications and the topographical peculiarities of the spot, and not without results. I discovered that the kraal was indeed impregnable to a front attack, but that it was very slightly defended to the rear, which ran up a slope of the mountain, indeed only by two lines of stone walls. The reason of this was that the mountain is quite impassable except by one secret path supposed to be known only to the chief and his councillors, and this being so, it had not been considered necessary to fortify it.

"'Well,' I said, when she had done, 'and now as to this secret path of thine—knowest thou aught of it?'

"'Ay,' she answered, 'I am no fool, Macumazahn. Knowledge learned is power earned. I won the secret of that path.'

"'And canst thou guide an impi thereon so that it shall fall upon the town from behind?'

"'Yes, I can do this, if only Wambe's people know not that the impi comes, for if they know, then they can block the way.'

"'So then here is my plan. Listen, Nala, and say if it be good, or if thou hast a better, show it forth. Let messengers go out and summon all thy impi, that it be gathered here on the third day from now. This being done, let the impi, led by Maiwa, march on the morrow of the fourth day, and crossing the mountains let it travel along on the other side of the mountains till it come to the place on the further side of which is the kraal of Wambe; that shall be some three days' journey in all. Then on the night of the third day's journey, let Maiwa lead the impi in silence up the secret path, so that it comes to the crest of the mountain that is above the strong place, and here let it hide among the rocks.

"'Meanwhile on the sixth day from now let one of thy Indunas, Nala, bring with him two hundred men that have guns, and lead me and my men as prisoners, and take also a girl from among the Butiana people, who by form and face is like unto Maiwa, and bind her hands, and pass by the road on which we came and through the cutting in the cliff on to the kraal of Wambe. But the men shall take no shields or plumes with them, only their guns and one short spear, and when they meet the people of Wambe they shall say that they come to give up the woman and the white man and his party to Wambe, and to make atonement to Wambe. So shall they pass in peace. And travelling thus, on the evening of the seventh day we shall come to the gates of the place of Wambe, and nigh the gates there is, so says Maiwa, a koppie very strong and full of rocks and caves, but having no soldiers on it except in time of war, or at the worst but a few such as can easily be overpowered.

"'This being done, at the dawn of day the impi on the mountain behind the town must light a fire and put wet grass on it, so that the smoke goes up. Then at the sight of the smoke we in the koppie will begin to shoot into the town of Wambe, and all the soldiers will run to kill us. But we will hold our own, and while we fight the impi shall charge down the mountain side and climb the schanses, and put those who defend them to the assegai, and then falling upon the town shall surprise it, and drive the soldiers of Wambe as a wind blows the dead husks of corn. This is my plan. I have spoken.'

"'*Ou!*' said Nala, 'it is good, it is very good. The white man is cleverer than a jackal. Yes, so shall it be; and may the snake of the Butiana people stand up upon its tail and prosper the war, for so shall we be rid of Wambe and the tyrannies of Wambe.'

"After that the girl Maiwa stood up, and once more producing the dreadful little dried hand, made her father and several of his head councillors swear by it and upon it that they would carry out the war of vengeance to the bitter end. It was a very curious sight to see. And by the way, the fight that ensued was thereafter known among the tribes of that district as the War of the Little Hand.

"The next two days were busy ones for us. Messengers were sent out, and every available man of the Butiana tribe was ordered up to 'a great dance.' The country was small, and by the evening of the second day, some twelve hundred and fifty men were assembled with their assegais and shields, and a fine hardy troop they were. At dawn of the following day, the fourth from the departure of the heralds, the main impi, having been doctored in the usual fashion, started under the command of Nala himself, who, knowing that his life and chieftainship hung upon the issue of the struggle, wisely determined to be present to direct it. With them went Maiwa, who was to guide them up the secret path. Of course we were obliged to give them two days' start, as they had more than a hundred miles of rough country to pass, including the crossing of the great mountain range which ran north and south, for it was necessary that the impi should make a wide détour in order to escape detection.

"At length, however, at dawn on the sixth day, I took the road, accompanied by my most unwilling bearers, who did not at all like the idea of thus putting their heads into the lion's mouth. Indeed, it was only the fear of Nala's spears, together with a vague confidence in myself, that induced them to accept the adventure. With me also were about two hundred Butianas, all armed with guns of various kinds, for many of these people had guns, though they were not very proficient in the use of them. But they carried no shields and wore no head-dress or armlets; indeed, every warlike appearance was carefully avoided. With our party went also a sister of Maiwa's, though by a different mother, who strongly resembled her in face and form, and whose mission it was to impersonate the runaway wife.

"That evening we camped upon the top of the cliff up which we had so barely escaped, and next morning at the first breaking of the light we rolled away the stones with which we had blocked the passage some days before, and descended to the hill-side beneath. Here the bodies, or rather the skeletons of the men who had fallen before my rifle, still lay about. The Matuku soldiers had left their comrades to be buried by the vultures. I descended the gully into which poor Gobo had fallen, and searched for his body, but in vain, although I found the spot where he and the other man had struck, together with the bones of the latter, which I recognized by the waist-cloth. Either some beast of prey had carried Gobo off, or the Matuku people had disposed of his remains, and also of my express rifle which he carried. At any rate, I never saw or heard any more of him.

"Once in Wambe's country, we adopted a very circumspect method of proceeding. About fifty men marched ahead in loose order to guard against surprise, while as many more followed behind. The remaining hundred were gathered in a bunch between, and in the centre of these men I marched, together with the girl who was personating Maiwa, and all my bearers. We were disarmed, and some of my men were tied together to show that we were prisoners, while the girl had a blanket thrown over her head, and moved along with an air of great dejection. We headed straight for Wambe's place, which was at a distance of about twenty-five miles from the mountain-pass.

"When we had gone some five miles we met a party of about fifty of Wambe's soldiers, who were evidently on the look-out for us. They stopped us, and their captain asked where we were going. The head man of our party answered that he was conveying Maiwa, Wambe's runaway wife, together with the white hunter and his men, to be given up to Wambe in accordance with his command. The captain then wanted to know why we were so many, to which our spokesman replied that I and my men were very desperate fellows, and that it was feared that if we were sent with a smaller escort we should escape, and bring disgrace and the wrath of Wambe upon their tribe. Thereon this gentleman, the Matuku captain, began to amuse himself at my expense, and mock me, saying that Wambe would make me pay for the soldiers whom I had killed. He would put me into the 'Thing that bites,' in other words, the lion trap, and leave me there to die like a jackal caught by the leg. I made no answer to this, though my wrath was great, but pretended to look frightened. Indeed there was not much pretence about it, I was frightened. I could not conceal from myself that ours was a most hazardous enterprise, and that it was very possible that I might make acquaintance with that lion trap before I was many days older. However, it seemed quite impossible to desert poor Every in his misfortune, so I had to go on, and trust to Providence, as I have so often been obliged to do before and since.

"And now a fresh difficulty arose. Wambe's soldiers insisted upon accompanying us, and what is more, did all they could to urge us forward, as they were naturally anxious to get to the chief's place before evening. But we, on the other hand, had excellent reasons for not arriving till night was closing in, since we relied upon the gloom to cover our advance upon the koppie which commanded the town. Finally, they became so importunate that we were obliged to refuse flatly to move faster, alleging as a reason that the girl was tired. They did not accept this excuse in good part, and at one time I thought that we should have come to blows, for there is no love lost between Butianas and Matukus. At last, however, either from motives of policy, or because they were so evidently outnumbered, they gave in and suffered us to go our own pace. I earnestly wished that they would have added to the obligation by going theirs, but this they declined absolutely to do. On the contrary, they accompanied us every foot of the way, keeping up a running fire of allusions to the 'Thing that bites' that jarred upon my nerves and discomposed my temper.

"About half-past four in the afternoon we came to a neck or ridge of stony ground, whence we could see Wambe's town plainly lying some six or seven miles away, and three thousand feet beneath us. The town is built in a valley, with the exception of Wambe's own kraal, that is situated at the mouth of some caves upon the slope of the opposing mountains, over which I hoped to see our impi's spears flashing in the morrow's light. Even from where we stood, it was easy to see how strongly the place was fortified with schanses and stone walls, and how difficult of approach. Indeed, unless taken by surprise, it seemed to me quite impregnable to a force operating without cannon, and even cannon would not make much impression on rocks and stony koppies filled with caves.

"Then came the descent of the pass, and an arduous business it was, for the path—if it may be called a path—is almost entirely composed of huge water-worn boulders, from the one to the other of which we must jump like so many grasshoppers. It took us two hours to climb down, and, travelling through that burning sun, when at last we did reach the bottom, I for one was nearly played out. Shortly afterwards, just as it was growing dark, we came to the first line of fortifications, which consisted of a triple stone wall pierced by a gateway, so narrow that a man could hardly squeeze through it. We passed this without question, being accompanied by Wambe's soldiers. Then, came a belt of land three hundred paces or more in width, very rocky and broken, and having no huts upon it. Here in hollows in this belt the cattle were kraaled in case of danger. On the further side were more fortifications and another small gateway shaped like a V, and just beyond and through it I saw the koppie we had planned to seize looming up against the line of mountains behind.

"As we went I whispered my suggestions to our captain, with the result that at the second gateway he halted the cavalcade, and addressing the captain of Wambe's soldiers, said that we would wait here till we received Wambe's word to enter the town. The other man said that this was well, only he must hand over the prisoners to be taken up to the chief's kraal, for Wambe, was 'hungry to begin upon them,' and his 'heart desired to see the white man at rest before he closed his eyes in sleep,' and as for his wife, 'surely he would welcome her.' Our leader replied that he could not do this thing, because his orders were to deliver the prisoners to Wambe at Wambe's own kraal, and they might not be broken. How could he be responsible for the safety of the prisoners if he let them out of his hand? No, they would wait there till Wambe's word was brought.

"To this, after some demur, the other man consented, and went away, remarking that he would soon be back. As he passed me he called out with a sneer, pointing as he did so to the fading red in the western sky—'Look your last upon the light, White Man, for the "Thing that bites" lives in the dark.'

"Next day it so happened that I shot this man, and, do you know, I think that he is about the only human being who has come to harm at my hands for whom I do not feel sincere sorrow and, in a degree, remorse.

The Attack

"Just where we halted ran a little stream of water. I looked at it, and an idea struck me: probably there would be no water on the koppie. I suggested this to our captain, and, acting on the hint, he directed all the men to drink what they could, and also to fill the seven or eight cooking pots which we carried with us with water. Then came the crucial moment. How were we to get possession of the koppie? When the captain asked me, I said that I thought that we had better march up and take it, and this accordingly we went on to do. When we came to the narrow gateway we were, as I expected stopped by two soldiers who stood on guard there and asked our business. The captain answered that we had changed our minds, and would follow on to Wambe's kraal. The soldiers said no, we must now wait.

"To this we replied by pushing them to one side and marching in single file through the gateway, which was not distant more than a hundred yards from the koppie. While we were getting through, the men we had pushed away ran towards the town calling for assistance, a call that was promptly responded to, for in another minute we saw scores of armed men running hard in our direction. So we ran too, for the koppie. As soon as they understood what we were after, which they did not at first, owing to the dimness of the light, they did their best to get there before us. But we had the start of them, and with the exception of one unfortunate man who stumbled and fell, we were well on to the koppie before they arrived. This man they captured, and when fighting began on the following morning, and he refused to give any information, they killed him. Luckily they had no time to torture him, or they would certainly have done so, for these Matuku people are very fond of torturing their enemies.

"When we reached the koppie, the base of which covers about half an acre of ground, the soldiers who had been trying to cut us off halted, for they knew the strength of the position. This gave us a few minutes before the light had quite vanished to reconnoitre the place. We found that it was unoccupied, fortified with a regular labyrinth of stone walls, and contained three large caves and some smaller ones. The next business was to post the soldiers to such advantage as time would allow. My own men I was careful to place quite at the top. They were perfectly useless from terror, and I feared that they might try to escape and give information of our plans to Wambe. So I watched them like the apple of my eye, telling them that should they dare to stir they would be shot.

"Then it grew quite dark, and presently out of the darkness I heard a voice—it was that of the leader of the soldiers who had escorted us—calling us to come down. We replied that it was too dark to move, we should hit our feet against the stones. He insisted upon our descending, and we flatly refused, saying that if any attempt was made to dislodge us we would fire. After that, as they had no real intention of attacking us in the dark, the men withdrew, but we saw from the fires which were lit around that they were keeping a strict watch upon our position.

"That night was a wearing one, for we never quite knew how the situation was going to develop. Fortunately we had some cooked food with us, so we did not starve. It was lucky, however, that we drunk our fill before coming up, for, as I had anticipated, there was not a drop of water on the koppie.

"At length the night wore away, and with the first tinge of light I began to go my rounds, and stumbling along the stony paths, to make things as ready as I could for the attack, which I felt sure would be delivered before we were two hours older. The men were cramped and cold, and consequently low-spirited, but I exhorted them to the best of my ability, bidding them remember the race from which they sprang, and not to show the white feather before a crowd of Matuku dogs. At length it began to grow light, and presently I saw long columns of men advancing towards the koppie. They halted under cover at a distance of about a hundred and fifty yards, and just as the dawn broke a herald came forward and called to us. Our captain stood up upon a rock and answered him.

"'These are the words of Wambe,' the herald said. 'Come forth from the koppie, and give over the evil-doers, and go in peace, or stay in the koppie and be slain.'

"'It is too early to come out as yet,' answered our man in fine diplomatic style. 'When the sun sucks up the mist then we will come out. Our limbs are stiff with cold.'

"'Come forth even now,' said the herald.

"'Not if I know it, my boy,' said I to myself; but the captain replied that he would come out when he thought proper, and not before.

"'Then make ready to die,' said the herald, for all the world like the villain of a transpontine piece, and majestically stalked back to the soldiers.

"I made my final arrangements, and looked anxiously at the mountain crest a couple of miles or so away, from which the mist was now beginning to lift, but no column of smoke could I see. I whistled, for if the attacking force had been delayed or made any mistake, our position was likely to grow rather warm. We had barely enough water to wet the mouths of the men, and when once it was finished we could not hold the place for long in that burning heat.

"At length, just as the sun rose in glory over the heights behind us, the Matuku soldiers, of whom about fifteen hundred were now assembled, set up a queer whistling noise, which ended in a chant. Then some shots were fired, for the Matuku had a few guns, but without effect, though one bullet passed just by a man's head.

"'Now they are going to begin,' I thought to myself, and I was not far wrong, for in another minute the body of men divided into three companies, each about five hundred strong, and, heralded by a running fire, charged at us on three sides. Our men were now all well under cover, and the fire did us no harm. I mounted on a rock so as to command a view of as much of the koppie and plain as possible, and yelled to our men to reserve their fire till I gave the word, and then to shoot low and load as quickly as possible. I knew that, like all natives, they were sure to be execrable shots, and that they were armed with weapons made out of old gas-pipes, so the only chance of doing execution was to let the enemy get right on to us.

"On they came with a rush; they were within eighty yards now, and as they drew near the point of attack, I observed that they closed their ranks, which was so much the better for us.

"'Shall we not fire, my father?' sung out the captain.

"'No, confound you!' I answered.

"'Sixty yards—fifty—forty—thirty. Fire, you scoundrels!' I yelled, setting the example by letting off both barrels of my elephant gun into the thickest part of the company opposite to me.

"Instantly the place rang out with the discharge of two hundred and odd guns, while the air was torn by the passage of every sort of missile, from iron pot legs down to slugs and pebbles coated with lead. The result was very prompt. The Matukus were so near that we could not miss them, and at thirty yards a lead-coated stone out of a gas-pipe is as effective as a Martini rifle, or more so. Over rolled the attacking soldiers by the dozen, while the survivors, fairly frightened, took to their heels. We plied them with shot till they were out of range—I made it very warm for them with the elephant gun, by the way—and then we loaded up in quite a cheerful frame of mind, for we had not lost a man, whereas I could count more than fifty dead and wounded Matukus. The only thing that damped my ardour was that, stare as I would, I could see no column of smoke upon the mountain crest.

"Half an hour elapsed before any further steps were taken against us. Then the attacking force adopted different tactics. Seeing that it was very risky to try to rush us in dense masses, they opened out into skirmishing order and ran across the open space in lots of five and six. As it happened, right at the foot of the koppie the ground broke away a little in such fashion that it was almost impossible for us to search it effectually with our fire. On the hither side of this dip Wambe's soldiers were now congregating in considerable numbers. Of course we did them as much damage as we could while they were running across, but this sort of work requires good shots, and that was just what we had not got. Another thing was, that so many of our men would insist upon letting off the things they called guns at every little knot of the enemy that ran across. Thus, the first few lots were indeed practically swept away, but after that, as it took a long while to load the gas-pipes and old flint muskets, those who followed got across in comparative safety. For my own part, I fired away with the elephant gun and repeating carbine till they grew almost too hot to hold, but my individual efforts could do nothing to stop such a rush, or perceptibly to lessen the number of our enemies.

"At length there were at least a thousand men crowded into the dip of ground within a few yards of us, whence those of them who had guns kept up a continued fusillade upon the koppie. They killed two of my bearers in this way, and wounded a third, for being at the top of the koppie these men were most exposed to the fire from the dip at its base. Seeing that the situation was growing most serious, at length, by the dint of threats and entreaties, I persuaded the majority of our people to cease firing useless shots, to reload, and prepare for the rush. Scarcely had I done so when the enemy came for us with a roar. I am bound to say that I should never have believed that Matukus had it in them to make such a determined charge. A large party rushed round the base of the koppie, and attacked us in flank, while the others swarmed wherever they could get a foothold, so that we were taken on every side.

"'*Fire!*' I cried, and we did with terrible effect. Many of their men fell, but though we checked we could not stop them. They closed up and rushed the first fortification, killing a good number of its defenders. It was almost all cold steel work now, for we had no time to reload, and that suited the Butiana habits of fighting well enough, for the stabbing assegai is a weapon which they understand. Those of our people who escaped from the first line of walls took refuge in the second, where I stood myself, encouraging them, and there the fight raged fiercely. Occasionally parties of the enemy would force a passage, only to perish on the hither side beneath the Butiana spears. But still they kept it up, and I saw that, fight as we would, we were doomed. We were altogether outnumbered, and to make matters worse, fresh bodies of soldiers were pouring across the plain to the assistance of our assailants. So I made up my mind to direct a retreat into the caves, and there expire in a manner as heroic as circumstances would allow; and while mentally lamenting my hard fate and reflecting on my sins I fought away like a fiend. It was then, I remember, that I shot my friend the captain of our escort of the previous day. He had caught sight of me, and making a vicious dig at my stomach with a spear (which I successfully dodged), shouted out, or rather began to shout out, one of his unpleasant allusions to the 'Thing that——' He never got as far as 'bites,' because I shot him after 'that.'

"Well, the game was about up. Already I saw one man throw down his spear in token of surrender—which act of cowardice cost him his life, by the way—when suddenly a shout arose.

"'Look at the mountain,' they cried; 'there is an impi on the mountain side.'

"I glanced up, and there sure enough, about half-way down the mountain, nearing the first fortification, the long-plumed double line of Nala's warriors was rushing down to battle, the bright light of the morning glancing on their spears. Afterwards we discovered that the reason of their delay was that they had been stopped by a river in flood, and could not reach the mountain crest by dawn. When they did reach it, however, they saw instantly that the fight was already going on, was 'in flower,' as they put it, and so advanced at once without waiting to light signal-fires.

"Meanwhile they had been observed from the town, and parties of soldiers were charging up the steep side of the hill, to occupy the schanses, and the second line of fortifications behind them. The first line they did not now attempt to reach or defend; Nala pressed them too close. But they got to the schanses or pits protected with stone walls, and constructed to hold from a dozen to twenty men, and soon began to open fire from them, and from isolated rocks. I turned my eyes to the gates of the town, which were placed to the north and south. Already they were crowded with hundreds of fugitive women and children flying to the rocks and caves for shelter from the foe.

"As for ourselves, the appearance of Nala's impi produced a wonderful change for the better in our position. The soldiers attacking us turned, realizing that the town was being assailed from the rear, and clambering down the koppie streamed off to protect their homes against this new enemy. In five minutes there was not a man left except those who would move no more, or were too sorely wounded to escape. I felt inclined to ejaculate '*Saved!*' like the gentleman in the play, but did not because the occasion was too serious. What I did do was to muster all the men and reckon up our losses. They amounted to fifty- one killed and wounded, sixteen men having been killed outright. Then I sent men with the cooking-pots to the stream of water, and we drank. This done I set my bearers, being the most useless part of the community, from a fighting point of view, to the task of attending the injured, and turned to watch the fray.

"By this time Nala's impi had climbed the first line of fortifications without opposition, and was advancing in a long line upon the schanses or pits which were scattered about between it and the second line, singing a war chant as it came. Presently puffs of smoke began to start from the schanses, and with my glasses I could see several of our men falling over. Then as they came opposite a schanse that portion of the long line of warriors would thicken up and charge it with a wild rush. I could see them leap on to the walls and vanish into the depths beneath, some of their number falling backward on each occasion, shot or stabbed to death.

"Next would come another act in the tragedy. Out from the hither side of the schanse would pour such of its defenders as were left alive, perhaps three or four and perhaps a dozen, running for dear life, with the war dogs on their tracks. One by one they would be caught, then up flashed the great spear and down fell the pursued—dead. I saw ten of our men leap into one large schanse, but though I watched for some time nobody came out. Afterwards we inspected the place and found these men all dead, together with twenty-three Matukus. Neither side would give in, and they had fought it out to the bitter end.

"At last they neared the second line of fortifications, behind which the whole remaining Matuku force, numbering some two thousand men, was rapidly assembling. One little pause to get their breath, and Nala's men came at it with a rush and a long wild shout of '*Bulala Matuku*' (kill the Matuku) that went right through me, thrilling every nerve. Then came an answering shout, and the sounds of heavy firing, and presently I saw our men retreating, somewhat fewer in numbers than they had advanced. Their welcome had been a warm one for the Matuku fight splendidly behind walls. This decided me that it was necessary to create a diversion; if we did not do so it seemed very probable that we should be worsted after all. I called to the captain of our little force, and rapidly put the position before him.

"Seeing the urgency of the occasion, he agreed with me that we must risk it, and in two minutes more, with the exception of my own men, whom I left to guard the wounded, we were trotting across the open space and through the deserted town towards the spot where the struggle was taking place, some seven hundred yards away. In six or eight minutes we reached a group of huts—it was a head man's kraal, that was situated about a hundred and twenty yards behind the fortified wall, and took possession of it unobserved. The enemy was too much engaged with the foe in front of him to notice us, and besides, the broken ground rose in a hog-back shape between. There we waited a minute or two and recovered our breath, while I gave my directions. So soon as we heard the Butiana impi begin to charge again, we were to run out in a line to the brow of the hogback and pour our fire into the mass of defenders behind the wall. Then the guns were to be thrown down and we must charge with the assegai. We had no shields, but that could not be helped; there would be no time to reload the guns, and it was absolutely necessary that the enemy should be disconcerted at the moment when the main attack was delivered.

"The men, who were as plucky a set of fellows as ever I saw, and whose blood was now thoroughly up, consented to this scheme, though I could see that they thought it rather a large order, as indeed I did myself. But I knew that if the impi was driven back a second time the game would be played, and for me at any rate it would be a case of the 'Thing that bites,' and this sure and certain knowledge filled my breast with valour.

"We had not long to wait. Presently we heard the Butiana war-song swelling loud and long; they had commenced their attack. I made a sign, and the hundred and fifty men, headed by myself, poured out of the kraal, and getting into a rough line ran up the fifty or sixty yards of slope that intervened between ourselves and the crest of the hog-backed ridge. In thirty seconds we were there, and immediately beyond us was the main body of the Matuku host waiting the onslaught of the enemy with guns and spears. Even now they did not see us, so intent were they upon the coming attack. I signed to my men to take careful aim, and suddenly called out to them to fire, which they did with a will, dropping thirty or forty Matukus.

"'*Charge!*' I shouted, again throwing down my smoking rifle and drawing my revolver, an example which they followed, snatching up their spears from the ground where they had placed them while they fired. The men set up a savage whoop, and we started. I saw the Matuku soldiers wheel around in hundreds, utterly taken aback at this new development of the situation. And looking over them, before we had gone twenty yards I saw something else. For of a sudden, as though they had risen from the earth, there appeared above the wall hundreds of great spears, followed by hundreds of savage faces shadowed with drooping plumes. With a yell they sprang upon the wall shaking their broad shields, and with a yell they bounded from it straight into our astonished foes.

"*Crash!* we were in them now, and fighting like demons. *Crash!* from the other side. Nala's impi was at its work, and still the spears and plumes appeared for a moment against the brown background of the mountain, and then sprang down and rushed like a storm upon the foe. The great mob of men turned this way and turned that way, astonished, bewildered, overborne by doubt and terror.

"Meanwhile the slayers stayed not their hands, and on every side spears flashed, and the fierce shout of triumph went up to heaven. There too on the wall stood Maiwa, a white garment streaming from her shoulders, an assegai in her hand, her breast heaving, her eyes flashing. Above all the din of battle I could catch the tones of her clear voice as she urged the soldiers on to victory. But victory was not yet. Wambe's soldiers gathered themselves together, and bore our men back by the sheer weight of numbers. They began to give, then once more they rallied, and the fight hung doubtfully.

"'Slay, you war-whelps,' cried Maiwa from the wall. 'Are you afraid, you women, you chicken-hearted women! Strike home, or die like dogs! What—you give way! Follow me, children of Nala.' And with one long cry she leapt from the wall as leaps a stricken antelope, and holding the spear poised rushed right into the thickest of the fray. The warriors saw her, and raised such a shout that it echoed like thunder against the mountains. They massed together, and following the flutter of her white robe crashed into the dense heart of the foe. Down went the Matuku before them like trees before a whirlwind. Nothing could stand in the face of such a rush as that. It was as the rush of a torrent bursting its banks. All along their line swept the wild desperate charge; and there, straight in the forefront of the battle, still waved the white robe of Maiwa.

"Then they broke, and, stricken with utter panic, Wambe's soldiers streamed away a scattered crowd of fugitives, while after them thundered the footfall of the victors.

"The fight was over, we had won the day; and for my part I sat down upon a stone and wiped my forehead, thanking Providence that I had lived to see the end of it. Twenty minutes later Nala's warriors began to return panting. 'Wambe's soldiers had taken to the bush and the caves,' they said, 'where they had not thought it safe to follow them,' adding significantly, that many had stopped on the way.

"I was utterly dazed, and now that the fight was over my energy seemed to have left me, and I did not pay much attention, till presently I was aroused by somebody calling me by my name. I looked up, and saw that it was the chief Nala himself, who was bleeding from a flesh wound in his arm. By his side stood Maiwa panting, but unhurt, and wearing on her face a proud and terrifying air.

"'They are gone, Macumazahn,' said the chief; 'there is little to fear from them, their heart is broken. But where is Wambe the chief?—and where is the white man thou camest to save?'

"'I know not,' I answered.

"Close to where we stood lay a Matuku, a young man who had been shot through the fleshy part of the calf. It was a trifling wound, but it prevented him from running away.

"'Say, thou dog,' said Nala, stalking up to him and shaking his red spear in his face, 'say, where is Wambe? Speak, or I slay thee. Was he with the soldiers?'

"'Nay, lord, I know not,' groaned the terrified man, 'he fought not with us; Wambe has no stomach for fighting. Perchance he is in his kraal yonder, or in the cave behind the kraal,' and he pointed to a small enclosure on the hillside, about four hundred yards to the right of where we were.

"'Let us go and see,' said Nala, summoning his soldiers.

Maiwa Is Avenged

"The impi formed up; alas, an hour before it had been stronger by a third than it was now. Then Nala detached two hundred men to collect and attend to the injured, and at my suggestion issued a stringent order that none of the enemy's wounded, and above all no women or children, were to be killed, as is the savage custom among African natives. On the contrary, they were to be allowed to send word to their women that they might come in to nurse them and fear nothing, for Nala made war upon Wambe the tyrant, and not on the Matuku tribe.

"Then we started with some four hundred men for the chief's kraal. Very soon we were there. It was, as I have said, placed against the mountain side, but within the fortified lines, and did not at all cover more than an acre and a half of ground. Outside was a tiny reed fence, within which, neatly arranged in a semi-circular line, stood the huts of the chief's principal wives. Maiwa of course knew every inch of the kraal, for she had lived in it, and led us straight to the entrance. We peeped through the gateway—not a soul was to be seen. There were the huts and there was the clear open space floored with a concrete of lime, on which the sun beat fiercely, but nobody could we see or hear.

"'The jackal has gone to earth,' said Maiwa; 'he will be in the cave behind his hut,' and she pointed with her spear towards another small and semi-circular enclosure, over which a large hut was visible, that had the cliff itself for a background. I stared at this fence; by George! it was true, it was entirely made of tusks of ivory planted in the ground with their points bending outwards. The smallest ones, though none were small, were placed nearest to the cliff on either side, but they gradually increased in size till they culminated in two enormous tusks, which, set up so that their points met, something in the shape of an inverted V, formed the gateway to the hut. I was dumbfoundered with delight; and indeed, where is the elephant-hunter who would not be, if he suddenly saw five or six hundred picked tusks set up in a row, and only waiting for him to take them away? Of course the stuff was what is known as 'black' ivory; that is, the exterior of the tusks had become black from years or perhaps centuries of exposure to wind and weather, but I was certain that it would be none the worse for that. Forgetting the danger of the deed, in my excitement I actually ran right across the open space, and drawing my knife scratched vigorously at one of the great tusks to see how deep the damage might be. As I thought, it was nothing; there beneath the black covering gleamed the pure white ivory. I could have capered for joy, for I fear that I am very mercenary at heart, when suddenly I heard the faint echo of a cry for assistance. 'Help!' screamed a voice in the Sisutu dialect from somewhere behind the hut; 'help! they are murdering me.'

"*I knew the voice*; it was John Every's. Oh, what a selfish brute was I! For the moment that miserable ivory had driven the recollection of him out of my head, and now—perhaps it was too late.

"Nala, Maiwa, and the soldiers had now come up. They too heard the voice and interpreted its tone, though they had not caught the words.

"'This way,' cried Maiwa, and we started at a run, passing round the hut of Wambe. Behind was the narrow entrance to a cave. We rushed through it heedless of the danger of the ambush, and this is what we saw, though very confusedly at first, owing to the gloom.

"In the centre of the cave, and with either end secured to the floor by strong stakes, stood a huge double-springed lion trap edged with sharp and grinning teeth. It was set, and beyond the trap, indeed almost over it, a terrible struggle was in progress. A naked or almost naked white man, with a great beard hanging down over his breast, in spite of his furious struggles, was being slowly forced and dragged towards the trap by six or eight women. Only one man was present, a fat, cruel-looking man with small eyes and a hanging lip. It was the chief Wambe, and he stood by the trap ready to force the victim down upon it so soon as the women had dragged him into the necessary position.

"At this instant they caught sight of us, and there came a moment's pause, and then, before I knew what she was going to do, Maiwa lifted the assegai she still held, and whirled it at Wambe's head. I saw the flash of light speed towards him, and so did he, for he stepped backward to avoid it—stepped backward right into the trap. He yelled with pain as the iron teeth of the 'Thing that bites' sprang up with a rattling sound like living fangs and fastened into him—such a yell I have not often heard. Now at last he tasted of the torture which he had inflicted upon so many, and though I trust I am a Christian, I cannot say that I felt sorry for him.

"The assegai sped on and struck one of the women who had hold of the unfortunate Every, piercing through her arm. This made her leave go, an example that the other women quickly followed, so that Every fell to the ground, where he lay gasping.

"'Kill the witches,' roared Nala, in a voice of thunder, pointing to the group of women.

"'Nay,' gasped Every, 'spare them. He made them do it,' and he pointed to the human fiend in the trap. Then Maiwa waved her hand to us to fall back, for the moment of her vengeance was come. We did so, and she strode up to her lord, and flinging the white robe from her stood before him, her fierce beautiful face fixed like stone.

"'Who am I?' she cried in so terrible a voice that he ceased his yells. 'Am I that woman who was given to thee for wife, and whose child thou slewest? Or am I an avenging spirit come to see thee die?

"'What is this?' she went on, drawing the withered baby-hand from the pouch at her side.

"'Is it the hand of a babe? and how came that hand to be thus alone? What cut it off from the babe? and where is the babe? Is it a hand? or is it the vision of a hand that shall presently tear thy throat?

"'Where are thy soldiers, Wambe? Do they sleep and eat and go forth to do thy bidding? or are they perchance dead and scattered like the winter leaves?'

"He groaned and rolled his eyes while the fierce-faced woman went on.

"'Art thou still a chief, Wambe? or does another take thy place and power, and say, Lord, what doest thou there? and what is that slave's leglet upon thy knee?

"'Is it a dream, Wambe, great lord and chief? or'—and she lifted her clenched hands and shook them in his face—'hath a woman's vengeance found thee out and a woman's wit o'ermatched thy tyrannous strength? and art thou about to slowly die in torments horrible to think on, oh, thou accursed murderer of little children?'

"And with one wild scream she dashed the dead hand of the child straight into his face, and then fell senseless on the floor. As for the demon in the trap, he shrank back so far as its iron bounds would allow, his yellow eyes starting out of his head with pain and terror, and then once more began to yell.

"The scene was more than I could bear.

"'Nala,' I said, 'this must stop. That man is a fiend, but he must not be left to die there. See thou to it.'

"'Nay," answered Nala, 'let him taste of the food wherewith he hath fed so many; leave him till death shall find him.'

"'That I will not,' I answered. 'Let his end be swift; see thou to it.'

"'As thou wilt, Macumazahn,' answered the chief, with a shrug of the shoulders; 'first let the white man and Maiwa be brought forth.'

"So the soldiers came forward and carried Every and the woman into the open air. As the former was borne past his tormentor, the fallen chief, so cowardly was his wicked heart, actually prayed him to intercede for him, and save him from a fate which, but for our providential appearance, would have been Every's own.

"So we went away, and in another moment one of the biggest villains on the earth troubled it no more. Once in the fresh air Every recovered quickly. I looked at him, and horror and sorrow pierced me through to see such a sight. His face was the face of a man of sixty, though he was not yet forty, and his poor body was cut to pieces with stripes and scars, and other marks of the torments which Wambe had for years amused himself with inflicting on him.

"As soon as he recovered himself a little he struggled on to his knees, burst into a paroxysm of weeping, and clasping my legs with his emaciated arms, would have actually kissed my feet.

"'What are you about, old fellow?' I said, for I am not accustomed to that sort of thing, and it made me feel uncomfortable.

"'Oh, God bless you?' he moaned, 'God bless you! If only you knew what I have gone through; and to think that you should have come to help me, and at the risk of your own life! Well, you were always a true friend—yes, yes, a true friend.'

"'Bosh,' I answered testily; 'I'm a trader, and I came after that ivory,' and I pointed to the stockade of tusks. 'Did you ever hear of an elephant-hunter who would not have risked his immortal soul for them, and much more his carcase?'

"But he took no notice of my explanations, and went on God blessing me as hard as ever, till at last I bethought me that a nip of brandy, of which I had a flask full, might steady his nerves a bit. I gave it him, and was not disappointed in the result, for he brisked up wonderfully. Then I hunted about in Wambe's hut, and found a kaross to put over his poor bruised shoulders, and he was quite a man again.

"'Now,' I said, 'why did the late lamented Wambe want to put you in that trap?'

"'Because as soon as they heard that the fight was going against them, and that Maiwa was charging at the head of Nala's impi, one of the women told Wambe that she had seen me write something on some leaves and give them to Maiwa before she went away to purify herself. Then of course he guessed that I had to do with your seizing the koppie and holding it while the impi rushed the place from the mountain, so he determined to torture me to death before help could come. Oh, heavens! what a mercy it is to hear English again.'

"'How long have you been a prisoner here, Every?' I asked.

"'Six years and a bit, Quatermain; I have lost count of the odd months lately. I came up here with Major Aldey and three other gentlemen and forty bearers. That devil Wambe ambushed us, and murdered the lot to get their guns. They weren't much use to him when he got them, being breech-loaders, for the fools fired away all the ammunition in a month or two. However, they are all in good order, and hanging up in the hut there. They didn't kill me because one of them saw me mending a gun just before they attacked us, so they kept me as a kind of armourer. Twice I tried to make a bolt of it, but was caught each time. Last time Wambe had me flogged very nearly to death—you can see the scars upon my back. Indeed I should have died if it hadn't been for the girl Maiwa, who nursed me by stealth. He got that accursed lion trap among our things also, and I suppose he has tortured between one and two hundred people to death in it. It was his favourite amusement, and he would go every day and sit and watch his victim till he died. Sometimes he would give him food and water to keep him alive longer, telling him or her that he would let him go if he lived till a certain day. But he never did let them go. They all died there, and I could show you their bones behind that rock.'

"'The devil!' I said, grinding my teeth. 'I wish I hadn't interfered; I wish I had left him to the same fate.'

"'Well, he got a taste of it any way,' said Every; 'I'm glad he got a taste. There's justice in it, and now he's gone to hell, and I hope there is another one ready for him there. By Jove! I should like to have the setting of it.'

"And so he talked on, and I sat and listened to him, wondering how he had kept his reason for so many years. But he didn't talk as I have told it, in plain English. He spoke very slowly, and as though he had got something in his mouth, continually using native words because the English ones had slipped his memory.

"At last Nala came up and told us that food was made ready, and thankful enough we were to get it, I can tell you. After we had eaten we held a consultation. Quite a thousand of Wambe's soldiers were put *hors de combat*, but at least two thousand remained hidden in the bush and rocks, and these men, together with those in the outlying kraals, were a source of possible danger. The question arose, therefore, what was to be done—were they to be followed or left alone? I waited till everybody had spoken, some giving one opinion and some another, and then being appealed to I gave mine. It was to the effect that Nala should take a leaf out of the great Zulu T'Chaka's book, and incorporate the tribe, not destroy it. We had a good many women among the prisoners. Let them, I suggested, be sent to the hiding-places of the soldiers and make an offer. If the men would come and lay down their arms and declare allegiance to Nala, they and their town and cattle should be spared. Wambe's cattle alone would be seized as the prize of war. Moreover, Wambe having left no children, his wife Maiwa should be declared chieftainess of the tribe, under Nala. If they did not accept this offer by the morning of the second day it should be taken as a declaration that they wished to continue the war. Their town should be burned, their cattle, which our men were already collecting and driving in in great numbers, would be taken, and they should be hunted down.

"This advice was at once declared to be wise, and acted on. The women were despatched, and I saw from their faces that they never expected to get such terms, and did not think that their mission would be in vain. Nevertheless, we spent that afternoon in preparations against possible surprise, and also in collecting all the wounded of both parties into a hospital, which we extemporized out of some huts, and there attending to them as best we could.

"That evening Every had the first pipe of tobacco that he had tasted for six years. Poor fellow, he nearly cried with joy over it. The night passed without any sign of attack, and on the following morning we began to see the effect of our message, for women, children, and a few men came in in little knots, and took possession of their huts. It was of course rather difficult to prevent our men from looting, and generally going on as natives, and for the matter of that white men too, are in the habit of doing after a victory. But one man who after warning was caught maltreating a woman was brought out and killed by Nala's order, and though there was a little grumbling, that put a stop to further trouble.

"On the second morning the head men and numbers of their followers came in in groups, and about midday a deputation of the former presented themselves before us without their weapons. They were conquered, they said, and Wambe was dead, so they came to hear the words of the great lion who had eaten them up, and of the crafty white man, the jackal, who had dug a hole for them to fall in, and of Maiwa, Lady of War, who had led the charge and turned the fate of the battle.

"So we let them hear the words, and when we had done an old man rose and said, that in the name of the people he accepted the yoke that was laid upon their shoulders, and that the more gladly because even the rule of a woman could not be worse than the rule of Wambe. Moreover, they knew Maiwa, the Lady of War, and feared her not, though she was a witch and terrible to see in battle.

"Then Nala asked his daughter if she was willing to become chieftainess of the tribe under him.

"Maiwa, who had been very silent since her revenge was accomplished, answered yes, that she was, and that her rule should be good and gentle to those who were good and gentle to her, but the froward and rebellious she would smite with a rod of iron; which from my knowledge of her character I thought exceedingly probable.

"The head man replied that that was a good saying, and they did not complain at it, and so the meeting ended.

"Next day we spent in preparations for departure. Mine consisted chiefly in superintending the digging up of the stockade of ivory tusks, which I did with the greatest satisfaction. There were some five hundred of them altogether. I made inquiries about it from Every, who told me that the stockade had been there so long that nobody seemed to know exactly who had collected the tusks originally. There was, however, a kind of superstitious feeling about them which had always prevented the chiefs from trying to sell this great mass of ivory. Every and I examined it carefully, and found that although it was so old its quality was really as good as ever, and there was very little soft ivory in the lot. At first I was rather afraid lest, now that my services had been rendered, Nala should hesitate to part with so much valuable property, but this was not the case. When I spoke to him on the subject he merely said, 'Take it, Macumazahn, take it; you have earned it well,' and, to speak the truth, though I say it who shouldn't, I think I had. So we pressed several hundred Matuku bearers into our service, and next day marched off with the lot.

"Before we went I took a formal farewell of Maiwa, whom we left with a bodyguard of three hundred men to assist her in settling the country. She gave me her hand to kiss in a queenly sort of way, and then said,

"'Macumazahn, you are a brave man, and have been a friend to me in my need. If ever you want help or shelter, remember that Maiwa has a good memory for friend and foe. All I have is yours.

"And so I thanked her and went. She was certainly a very remarkable woman. A year or two ago I heard that her father Nala was dead, and that she had succeeded to the chieftainship of both tribes, which she ruled with great justice and firmness.

"I can assure you that we ascended the pass leading to Wambe's town with feelings very different from those with which we had descended it a few days before. But if I was grateful for the issue of events, you can easily imagine what poor Every's feelings were. When we got to the top of the pass, before the whole impi he actually flopped down upon his knees and thanked Heaven for his escape, the tears running down his face. But then, as I have said, his nerves were shaken—though now that his beard was trimmed and he had some sort of clothes on his back, and hope in his heart, he looked a very different man from the poor wretch whom we had rescued from death by torture.

"Well, we separated from Nala at the little stairway or pass over the mountain—Every and I and the ivory going down the river which I had come up a few weeks before, and the chief returning to his own kraal on the further side of the mountain. He gave us an escort of a hundred and fifty men, however, with instructions to accompany us for six days' journey, and to keep the Matuku bearers in order and then return. I knew that in six days we should be able to reach a district where porters were plentiful, and whence we could easily get the ivory conveyed to Delagoa Bay."

"And did you land it up safe?" I asked.

"Well no," said Quatermain, "we lost about a third of it in crossing a river. A flood came down suddenly just as the men were crossing and many of them had to throw down their tusks to save their lives. We had no means of dragging it up, and so we were obliged to leave it, which was very sad. However, we sold what remained for nearly seven thousand pounds, so we did not do so badly. I don't mean that I got seven thousand pounds out of it, because, you see, I insisted upon Every taking a half share. Poor fellow, he had earned it, if ever a man did. He set up a store in the old colony on the proceeds and did uncommonly well."

"And what did you do with the lion trap?" asked Sir Henry.

"Oh, I brought that away with me also, and when I reached Durban I put it in my house. But really I could not bear to sit opposite to it at nights as I smoked. Visions of that poor woman and the hand of her dead child would rise up in my mind, and also of all the horrors of which it had been the instrument. I began to dream at last that it held me by the leg. This was too much for my nerves, so I just packed it up and shipped it to its maker in England, whose name was stamped upon the steel, sending him a letter at the same time to tell him to what purpose the infernal machine had been put. I believe that he gave it to some museum or other."

"And what became of the tusks of the three bulls which you shot! You must have left them at Nala's kraal, I suppose."

The old gentleman's face fell at this question.

"Ah," he said, "that is a very sad story. Nala promised to send them with my goods to my agent at Delagoa, and so he did. But the men who brought them were unarmed, and, as it happened, they fell in with a slave caravan under the command of a half-bred Portuguese, who seized the tusks, and what is worse, swore that he had shot them. I paid him out afterwards, however," he added with a smile of satisfaction, "but it did not give me back my tusks, which no doubt have been turned into hair brushes long ago;" and he sighed.

"Well," said Good, "that is a capital yarn of yours, Quatermain, but——"

"But what?" he asked sharply, foreseeing a draw.

"But I don't think that it was so good as mine about the ibex—it hasn't the same *finish*."

Mr. Quatermain made no reply. Good was beneath it.

"Do you know, gentlemen," he said, "it is half-past two in the morning, and if we are going to shoot the big wood to-morrow we ought to leave here at nine-thirty sharp."

"Oh, if you shoot for a hundred years you will never beat the record of those three woodcocks," I said.

"Or of those three elephants," added Sir Henry.

And then we all went to bed, and I dreamed that I had married Maiwa, and was much afraid of that attractive but determined lady.

www.ingramcontent.com/pod-product-compliance
Lightning Source LLC
Chambersburg PA
CBHW030415310726
48979CB00002B/421

* 9 7 9 8 8 8 0 9 0 1 4 3 2 *